A Flower
—— *of* ——
Love

A Flower
— of —
Love

Krister Hill

*i*Universe

A Flower of Love

Copyright © 2015 Krister Hill.

All rights reserved. No part of this book may be used or reproduced by any means, graphic, electronic, or mechanical, including photocopying, recording, taping or by any information storage retrieval system without the written permission of the publisher except in the case of brief quotations embodied in critical articles and reviews.

iUniverse books may be ordered through booksellers or by contacting:

iUniverse
1663 Liberty Drive
Bloomington, IN 47403
www.iuniverse.com
1-800-Authors (1-800-288-4677)

Because of the dynamic nature of the Internet, any web addresses or links contained in this book may have changed since publication and may no longer be valid. The views expressed in this work are solely those of the author and do not necessarily reflect the views of the publisher, and the publisher hereby disclaims any responsibility for them.

Any people depicted in stock imagery provided by Thinkstock are models, and such images are being used for illustrative purposes only. Certain stock imagery © Thinkstock.

ISBN: 978-1-4917-5905-9 (sc)
ISBN: 978-1-4917-5904-2 (e)

Library of Congress Control Number: 2015911011

Print information available on the last page.

iUniverse rev. date: 7/27/2015

Acknowledgements

I would like to thank my wife for all of the encouragement and love she has given me to finish this book.

For our children, the happiness and satisfaction of our lives.

I want to thank Raija and Camilla for always helping and being a support.

Special thanks to Raili and Harri for always being there for me, whether it shines or rains.

Last but First, I want to thank God, from the bottom of my heart, for making this book a reality.

Contents

Acknowledgements v
Prologue 1
1. While He Lay Dying...3
2. Toby the Elephant..7
3. A Little Girl and New Hope................................. 11
4. A Desire to Be a Father... 19
5. Restoring My Life.. 37
6. A Letter of Forgiveness... 53
7. To Care for One Another..................................... 59
8. Quality Time in the Big City............................... 65
9. An Elephant Ride and a Big Surprise 103
10. Planning for the Future....................................... 119
11. The Family Reunion.. 141
12. They Are No Longer Two But One 183
13. Love Like Nothing Else....................................... 189
14. A Friend Who Will Be Missed........................... 193

Prologue

John was running to save his life. He didn't know if he would see tomorrow. His heart filled with fear and despair. Men were shooting at him. He ran toward the jungle for protection. His adrenaline kept him from feeling the pain of the bullet passing through his upper body. Instead, he ran even faster with blood flowing down his arm. John reached the edge of the jungle with his strength slowly fading. His steps felt heavy.

He realized that his escape had cost him a bullet.

Willpower was all he had to keep running through the jungle depths. The blood loss took its toll and he fell to the ground. With his eyes fixed on the trees, John took deep breaths to remain conscious. He had no idea if his enemy had given up the chase.

John heard something coming toward him.

He prayed, "Oh God, please don't let me die like this." He was sure that at any second his life was over. He was stunned to see that the sound was coming from an elephant with a little girl on its back.

John had no idea, then, that these two would change his destiny forever.

While He Lay Dying

"Who is this little girl?" he thought to himself.

The last thing he remembered was the elephant's trunk lifting the girl down from its back and setting her right in front of him. The weakness from the blood loss caused him to pass out.

While lying there unconscious, the girl examined him and found the bullet wound in his upper chest. It had just missed his lung. Seeing that the bullet went right through his body, she grabbed her bag and took out some special herbs. She put these herbs on the entrance and exit holes of the bullet. The herbs stopped the bleeding. The girl instructed the elephant to pick him up and carry him on its back.

The elephant started to walk through the thick jungle toward their home. Pausing to take a break after awhile, the elephant set him down, laying him on top of a bed made of big jungle leaves. He was slowly coming back to consciousness.

Sensing that the elephant liked him, he began to pet its trunk with a thankful heart for being alive. While the elephant and he shared this moment of affection, a girl came out of the jungle and walked toward him. She wore a long, dirty, flower-print dress.

She walked up next to him and looked right into his eyes. He reached out his arms toward her and gave her a hug. Not being able to control his feelings, he cried tears of joy from his heart, realizing that God had really answered his prayer. He had given him another chance to live, to continue with his life.

With his eyes closed, he daydreamed that he was hugging this girl back at home, in front of his wife, telling her, "This girl saved my life."

He opened his eyes, back to reality, and thought to himself, This wonderful little girl must have some nice parents waiting for her.

He expected that they would not understand each other's language and was surprised to discover that this girl spoke very good English without any accent. Thank God she speaks English, he thought to himself.

"I'd like to introduce myself; my name is John Campbell."

"My name is Florence Anderson," she replied.

"Are your parents from Europe?" he asked.

"My parents came from England to India fifteen years ago to have their own business here," Florence said.

"What are you doing in the jungle by yourself?" he asked Florence.

With a surprising answer, Florence told him, "Same as you, running away and trying to survive, by letting no one know where I am."

Then she told him, "Two men came to rob my parents

at our house at the edge of the jungle. They killed my father and mother. I watched my parents from a distance, how the bad guys shot my parents. Then they put their bodies back inside the house and set it on fire. It has almost been a year since they killed my parents.

"My father had an import-export business for many years in India, and that's how I came to born here in India. I have an older brother named Jack. He serves in the navy and probably doesn't even know what has happened to our parents."

Toby the Elephant

John was curious about Florence. "How is it possible for you to make it in the jungle by yourself for so long?" he asked her.

Florence replied, "Don't forget that I am not alone. My elephant, Toby, has always been by my side and keeps me safe in the jungle. I never go in the jungle without riding him. This protects me from other wild animals. Other animals are fearful of Toby. I guess it's because he's so big."

She continued, "You're probably wondering how I ended up with Toby. So let me tell you John, how this dear friend came into my life.

"I met Toby the day I ran into the jungle to hide from the bad guys who killed my parents. When I found him, he was dying. He was stuck in muck. The muck reached up to his belly and he couldn't get out of the hole on his own. Our eyes locked and I realized that we both had something in common: The fear of death.

"For a while, we just looked at each other, wondering who the other was. Then all a sudden, I heard a voice in my head saying, 'Please help me. Don't let me die like this.' Toby's spirit and mine became one, because we both had the desire to live. I stopped thinking about my own survival and began to fight to save his life.

"I can't explain this. Running away and fearing for my life, and in the middle of everything, I stopped running and began to save someone else's life. I began to think hard about how I could get this big elephant out of the mucky hole. My first thought was to throw big leaves and little branches by his feet and try to make the muck less mucky. It worked; he was slowly able to move his feet more freely. But he still needed help to get out of the hole.

"I got him to grab the branch I was holding with his trunk. Then I pulled. Since he is so much heavier than myself, I guess you can imagine what happened in a tug-of-war between him and me, and who came out the winner.

"I had to come up with a new idea. He was stuck. He couldn't reach the tree branches on his own to pull himself out. Finally, I came up with a great idea. What if I make a rope? I could tie it around a big tree and toss it to him. He could grab it with his trunk and be able to pull himself out of the hole. I began to work on my idea.

"My father loved animals and nature. He once told me that nature provides everything you need in order to survive. My father taught me how to make a rope out of jungle vines. Depending on how thick the vines are, you can take a few and braid them together as you would braid human hair. So I finished braiding vines into a long rope and then tied the rope around a big tree. Then I tossed the other end of the rope to his trunk and he pulled himself out of the hole. I was so happy! I had never before felt this good in my life.

"I believe that I felt so good inside because I had made the right choice. Instead of thinking of myself, I stopped and helped someone else. The most beautiful thing about it all was that it didn't cost me a thing. All I did was offer my love to him and he accepted my help.

"In return, I received a friend for life and I named him Toby. He hugged me with his trunk. I looked into his eyes and hugged his head and began to cry. Then I remembered the situation I was running from. It hit me that I'd never be able to see my parents again, because they were now dead. Toby and I just stood there, crying tears together, not knowing what to do or where to go.

"Then Toby directed me to get up on his back. As soon as I was sitting on his back he began to walk toward the heart of the jungle. I felt safe on Toby's back. Even though I didn't know where he was taking me, I quickly accepted his companionship. I knew that I needed his protection to survive in this wild jungle. I rode that way for hours, deeper into unknown areas of the jungle. Suddenly, I noticed something covered by vines and leaves.

"It turned out to be an old abandoned temple from a long time ago. Toby and I cleaned the temple up and made it our home. We have been living on what the jungle has to offer. Mostly we eat fruit. Once a week we go fishing. I catch fish by spear hunting from Toby's back while he stands in the water. The river where we fish is about a two-hour ride from the temple.

"Next to my parents' house, my father built a guesthouse, combined with a shed for the tools necessary to maintain the grounds around the house. So of course, I have gone carefully back to this guesthouse a few times with Toby. We've collected items like clothing, an axe, a machete, along with many other things, which has helped me to survive in the jungle."

A Little Girl
and New Hope

"John, would you like to see our temple?" Florence asked. Of course he did. So they left and continued their journey toward the temple. Sitting with Florence on Toby's back, John felt that he needed to get to know Florence a little bit more.

So he said, "I hope you don't mind if I ask you a personal question."

"Of course not John, you can ask me anything."

"Well, this is my question. What are your plans for your future? You can't live in the jungle all your life; there is so much more to see of the world."

Florence answered, "I really haven't given it much thought. You are the first person I have talked to since my parents' deaths."

He reached into the chest pocket of his jacket and took out a picture of he and his wife. Florence looked at the picture for a moment and began to cry. "I'm so sorry for making you cry! You must've been through a lot during your time in the jungle, without any adults to help you. How can you ever forget the blessing of having wonderful parents and being part of a happy family?"

Then he asked Florence, "Have you ever been to England?"

She shook her head saying, "No."

"Would you like to come to England with me and meet my wife, Sarah? I know that I can never replace your father, but it would mean a lot to me if you would give me a chance to provide for you as a father would and to be your friend. After all, you have saved my life Florence. I can see that you have a lot of thoughts going on in your head right now. You don't have to answer me right now. You can answer later."

"What you just said reminds me of something my father once told me, not too long before the day he was killed. On that day I couldn't understand what my father was talking about, but right now I understand what he was saying. Simon, my father, spoke to me with these words. 'True success in life is not a matter of collecting things of the world, but instead of giving to the world without having anything of it.'

"Today I understand what he was trying to tell me, after hearing what you just said to me. In other words, he meant that when your personal time is put toward other people first, then you truly live for others."

"I can tell that your father must been a man filled with wisdom, as rich as your words are," he said to Florence. "By the way, how old are you?"

"I am twelve years-old."

"By the way you speak, you appear much older than your age."

Then she said to him, "Well you can imagine how different my lifestyle has become, living in the jungle. I was once a little girl playing around, cared for by my parents. Now I have to take care of myself and always be alert to stay alive from whatever would attack me in the jungle. I go to sleep every night in the pitch-black with only the firepit as a nightlight.

"It has been almost a year since I left my childhood. In many ways I have had to become an adult to stay alive. So yes, being in the jungle on my own, I have matured a lot for my age.

"My father was a great man John, not because of what he had, but because of how he loved all people. If someone asked for his help or advice, he would literally drop what he was doing and right away begin to help the person. My father had a saying that I liked a lot and it went like this: 'Life is not built on what you can see, but rather on what you are willing to believe in.'

"My parents were truly believers in God. They were raised as Christian believers and lived by the Word of God. The love of my parents and the way they lived it out, how loving they were toward all people, has also made me a Christian believer.

"I remember one time, when this scared-looking boy from a poor family came and asked my father to help him fix the flat tire on his bicycle. His bicycle was his whole family's pride and joy. They loved taking turns riding and enjoying it. The boy begged my father, 'Please help me fix the flat tire! I don't want to go home with the news that I've taken away the joy of our bike riding.'

"'Of course,' my father said, and helped him.

"As the boy was leaving my father to go home after the tire was fixed, my father said to me, 'Look at that. What a difference we can make and all it took was fifteen minutes of my time.' Then my father said to me, 'That was truly rewarding, to be able to turn a distraught face into a smiling face.'"

They continued through the jungle on Toby's back, only stopping for a short water break by a little creek that ran through the jungle. Standing on the elephant's back, John was able to reach some nice fruit up high in the trees. When they sat down by the creek to refresh themselves with the fruit and water, he started to admire the beautiful jungle. There were many flowers showing off their beauty and amazing colors wherever they looked. Butterflies flitted here and there, drinking the nectar of the jungle's flowers.

John had never seen so many butterflies in the same place with so many different shapes, forms, and colors as in that jungle. There were also many different kinds of insects that he had never seen before. Having the advantage of riding on the back of an elephant, he could see things from high up, things he wouldn't have been able to see if he had been walking on his own feet. They were also able to see many kinds of animals, like birds and monkeys. Florence also shared with John that there were wild tigers in this jungle.

"That's why we always have to stay close to Toby and his protection. Being on his back helps keeps us safe against the wild animals that may come close to us."

They continued their break by the creek, sitting on a fallen tree trunk, admiring the different sounds of the jungle. Florence then asked John, "Where are you from and what are you doing in this jungle by yourself?"

"Yes, it's time that I tell you the facts about my situation. I was born and raised in England, and have lived there all my life. I have two brothers and a sister and I am the youngest. My father's name is Philip and my mother's name is Susan. As far as I can remember, our family has always been involved in the military. My father is a retired general, but he is still involved in decision-making with the military. He served a long time and therefore has a lot of experience.

"My mother has always been a housewife and therefore we were raised mostly by her, because of my father's profession. Our mother gave us love and our father taught us what we could handle regarding discipline. As kids we didn't understand the importance of discipline and what comes from it. We were fearful at times and felt tense when our mother shouted, 'Daddy is home!' Whenever our father was home we couldn't sleep late in the morning.

He used to say, 'There are things to be done and it will not be done if you sleep more than you have to.' So you can imagine us all smiling every time our father left for work.

"His job took him away for days at time. But it's because of our strict upbringing that we are all doing well today. We understand the importance of having certain qualities in life, like respect, dignity, and honesty and that it all comes from discipline. Being raised with discipline in your life helps you to learn to stand on your own feet at early age."

Florence cut in and said to John, "I would love to hear more, but we must be going before we lose all daylight.

Believe me John, you don't want to be lost in the dark with wild animals all around." After filling up all water supply bottles, Florence and John climbed up on Toby's back and continued their journey toward the temple.

"Go ahead and continue your story. We have about an hour before we reach our destination."

So he continued, "I am here all alone just because of my own foolishness and self-pity. My wife, Sarah, and I have tried to have a child for almost two years. We have been to all kinds of doctors and when the truth was revealed to us, that I am the reason why we can't have a child, I didn't handle it very well. I realized that I couldn't give her what she desires the most. I can't give her a child, and therefore, her own family. She has dreamed about having her own family since she was a young teenager. I couldn't deal with the news that because of me, my wife's dream had to end. Instead of facing our options, I became blind and selfish. I needed to get away from everything. So I signed up to work for the United Nations as border patrol for six months.

"I was placed on the borders of India and Pakistan. I witnessed an attack against a village in Pakistan because of religious beliefs. A few Christians had moved into this village and began to teach about the Christian faith. Pakistan is a Muslim country and a few became upset and offended by these Christians and their beliefs. An uproar broke out, which became very violent, and lives were in danger. Because of the attack, I got involved as well, with open-fire to protect others and myself. Being out-numbered and therefore over-powered, I had no choice but to run for safety.

"I was running away when I got shot in the chest. Even so, I was still able to continue my escape. Then you ran into me, Florence, while I was lying on my back, asking God to spare me. I want to thank you for being so brave and for saving my life. I feel so foolish right now. I admire you for being so strong and not giving up, even when you lost the ones most precious to you, your parents.

"Look at me, Florence. I ran away from my wife and family... for what? Because I didn't like the situation I was in? But it didn't give me the right to bring more pain and suffering into my wife's life, by running away. I hope there is still time to make things right again between her and me. She has been writing to me every week since I left, but I haven't written back regularly. It took me three months before I picked up a pen and wrote to let her know that I was okay.

"I have been angry and bitter toward God for not letting me be able to give my wife a child. I must be honest with you, Florence. I admit that I am a rich and spoiled man and I have always gotten what I wanted. So for the first time in my life, when something didn't go my way, I ran away from everything, instead of being a man and dealing with the truth. That is the reason I am here today."

"Forgive me for changing the subject," Florence started, "However, there is a question I have wanted to ask you since we first met. Do you believe that God speaks to us? The reason I ask is because of this. Yesterday morning, early at the sunrise while waking up, I got a strong urge to explore further north of the jungle than I ever have before. Something kept me going further and further up north, until I ran into you, John. Then the sensation to keep going left me. So, do you think it was God telling me to go and save your life?"

"To be honest with you," he said, "Six months ago I would've answered you 'No,' but today I must say 'Yes.' Because of having so much time away from close family members, I began to long for a friend to talk to and to share my feelings with. Back home in England, I thought I knew God enough by going to church every Sunday and listening to the priest speaking about God. Because I felt so terribly lonely and didn't have anyone I felt comfortable talking to, I began to seek God and build a relationship with Him by reading the Bible- the Word of God. As I kept on reading the Bible every day and believing in what I read, my faith in God grew stronger day by day. I have never felt such peace in my heart. It surpasses my human understanding and I know that it's God giving it to me, because of the relationship I have in him. My mother always told me that the only way you will ever know God is to read the Bible. I thought I knew God but I was wrong.

"How can any relationship grow stronger, unless you spend time together and find out the truth about each other's strength and weaknesses? God says that anyone who knows Him will trust in Him. I trust my wife because I know her. I wish I knew God many years ago like I know Him today. So yes, I believe He spoke to you as well as He spoke to me, to come and patrol the border, in order for me to be found in Him and He in me."

A Desire to Be a Father

"When we met, Florence, I felt something strong in my spirit and therefore I feel drawn to you for some reason, even if I don't understand why right now."

"I feel the same way about you, too. I'm happy that we met. I haven't been able to speak to anyone like this since my parents died."

A blast from Toby's trunk interrupted them.

John asked Florence, "What's going on with Toby?"

"He's excited because our home is just behind the hill in front of us, where the temple is located."

As they reached the top of the hill and began to go downhill, they entered an opening in a stone wall, part of the old abandoned temple. As they entered the amazing temple yard, John felt like they were entering a new, beautiful world that he had never seen before in his whole entire life. There was an arrangement of flowers in colors so beautiful that it made him speechless.

Toby stopped walking. They both climbed down onto solid ground. John was in awe of the beauty all around them. Alarmed, Florence asked him, "Are you okay, John?" Speechless, he nodded his head and kept admiring the scenery of the most beautiful trees and flowers ever arranged by a human hand. As his eyes continued to explore the scenery around him, he fixated on the center of the courtyard's floor. The floor was dressed with flat stones in different sizes and colors all mixed together beautifully. It looked like there was once a big statue placed in the center made out of stone. All that was left of the statue were its feet.

Someone had placed round stones in a circle around the statue's feet, with a diameter of about three meters. Soil had been placed inside the circle.

Between the two feet of the old statue, a tree had been planted. The tree stood about three meters high. Around its base, inside the circle, flowers in many different colors were placed. There were also beautiful orchids that were circling around the base of the tree. The tree had no flowers of its own. Orchids in many different colors, shapes, and sizes had been grafted into the tree's branches, making it look like a tree with its own flowers.

John had never seen a tree made so beautifully by someone's hand. Every orchid was alive with the tree as though they were one. As he admired this place and its surroundings, he began to get sleepy. John began to feel the weakness of losing so much blood and fell asleep as he admired this beautiful tree and began to dream about his wife, Sarah.

In the dream, he saw himself back in England with his wife and Florence having a big welcome-home party with his whole family. The celebration was for his return home and the reunion with his wife. Everyone wondered, 'Who is that little girl?' John kept on dreaming with a smile on his face as the sun began to go down.

While he was sleeping, Florence started a fire in the fireplace in the courtyard. As the daylight disappeared and the darkness of the night began, John awoke to the smell of food being cooked over the fire. Once awake he noticed noises from the jungle that he couldn't hear during the day. Feeling a little fearful, he noticed Toby and Florence sitting close to the fire. The sight of them made him feel safe.

John stood up, walked toward Florence, and said, "Whatever you're cooking smells really good. I'm starving."

"Well, I hope you like chicken soup."

"Yes I do, but where did you get it?"

"I didn't share this with you earlier because I wanted to surprise you with some good food for dinner. My father stored lots of canned foods 'for a rainy day' in the shed by their house."

"I'm glad that your father planned for a rainy day, because I like this surprise a lot."

"I'm glad that you like my surprise. I made a few cans so we all can eat ourselves full and hopefully be able to sleep good tonight." Enjoying the food and feeling safe, they both ate and enjoyed the time together around the fire, the only thing that gave them light in the darkness of the night. Full and satisfied they fell asleep for the night.

John woke up first. It was sunrise and he realized how blessed he was to have Florence and her beautiful elephant friend, Toby, which was such an asset to have in the jungle. Not only that, but Toby made a great companion for them both.

While John was lying with the sun against his face, he began to thank God in prayer for bringing these two into his life. After he finished praying, he opened his eyes and Florence said to him, "Isn't it nice to have a relationship with God where you can speak to Him first, every new morning of the life He has blessed you with? And by doing so, you walk in thankfulness with His love in your heart guiding you through the day. Just like you, being on my own except for Toby, I sought God and learned to trust Him. Having Him alone as a friend has made me rely on Him completely. I know that He will always be by my side."

"I love my relationship with God," John replied to Florence. Looking around the courtyard again, he said "I would like to meet the person who has done all this beautiful work."

"You are looking at that person," Florence said.

"Where? I don't see them."

"Right here, are you blind?"

"You mean… you've done all this?" he asked her, incredulous.

"Yes, why is that so hard to believe?"

"Well, who moved those big trees out of the way?"

"Toby did," she said, laughing.

John had a hard time believing her. "I've never seen an elephant work, but I've heard that they are very strong animals. But that strong?"

"That strong," Florence said, looking around the garden. "And since my mother was a housewife, we had lots of time together working in our own garden and making it as beautiful as we could. Many times my father returned from a business trip, my mother and I loved to show him what we had done together in the garden. It became a way for us to express our love to him. My father couldn't wait to come home and see how the new garden looked. So I have had lots of practice.

"As far as I remember, my mother and I kept on doing this with the garden. She taught me everything I know about flowers." Florence paused to look at John. "Do you believe me now?"

"Yes I do, and I also believe that God has given you a wonderful gift, to work and arrange flowers. I can remember all of the weddings I've attended, and how much more beautiful they all would have been, if you had done the flower arrangements. I want you to know that you can get a job anywhere in this world arranging flowers." John thought a moment about everything... this setting, the young girl, this whole experience. "Since your name is Florence, and you love flowers so much, would you mind if I give you a nickname? Can I call you Flower?"

"I don't mind at all. Actually, I like the name a lot."

"I have a question for you, Flower." John stopped to smile at the sound of her nickname. "It's obvious that you love flowers, but my question is... why? I mean, I know they remind you of time with your parents... but doesn't that make them painful?"

"That's an easy question to answer, John. Flowers are similar to humans; a flower that is lacking light will slowly die. Without light, all living things will die. For human beings, light means love. Love brings out the best in all of us. My father and I used to talk about love all the time and how it affects us in a good way. He used to say, 'Remember, a man's reflection is revealed by a man's actions.' In other words, what's in a man's heart will become his actions. I have seen many depressed children because of love lacking in their lives.

"I have also seen many children full of life, because of the love that their parents give them. So I have seen both sides of life, with love and without love. I have come to understand the importance of having love in our lives, for it brings light into our lives. So it's the same with a flower that is planted in a dark place. By moving a flower into a lighter place, you give it another chance to grow.

"Your parents must have been very wise. You speak with such wisdom for being so young," John said. "By the way Flower, when is your birthday?"

"My birthday is on Christmas day. My parents told me that I was the best gift they had ever received for Christmas." He looked at his watch.

"Today is the first day of December and my first Christmas month without being beside my wife. Oh… I miss her so much."

"You must write to her right away, John. I know where to go so you can write and mail her a letter. I can take you to a little town not far from here. You will find what you need to write a letter to your wife. I haven't been there since my parents were alive. I've been afraid that the men who killed my parents might be there. And I'm not sure if they saw me watching them commit murder. But maybe, having you with me, I'll feel safe to go back again."

"Of course I will go with you, Flower." John continued looking around the temple and its surroundings from where he'd left off yesterday when he fell asleep. Sitting inside a square of four walls, of different sized stones, he realized what a unique place this was and how much more beautiful it must have been, before someone came and destroyed it all. He guessed that the broken walls were each about twenty-five meters long. The walls were about a meter thick and only three meters high. By looking at the fallen stones next to the wall, he guessed the walls used to be double in height, before being destroyed. In each corner inside the temple walls you could see the remains of a statue, also made out of stones. John couldn't make out how these statues used to look because of the severe damage to them.

There was only one way into the temple, and it was located in the center of one of the walls. From what he could see lying on the ground next to the entrance, he would say that there used to be a big wooden gate to complete the walls. Whoever was inside the gate was safe against whatever was on the outside.

Then something interesting caught his eyes.

All of the fallen stones were lying outside the temple on the ground.

This meant that the walls were destroyed from the inside-out and not from the outside-in. Maybe there was a rebellion inside the temple? Not far from the tree in the center of the courtyard was a well for water. Whoever destroyed the temple also filled the well with stones. Someone was very angry with this place and its gods. John liked the bed that Flower had made, with old wood from the gate as a box spring. It kept one off the ground and dry in rain. The cushion of big jungle leaves made it nice and soft to sleep on.

He also liked the little roof that Flower had built. She wisely used the wall as a foundation to build the roof in order to keep dry when it rained. He could see that she placed two trees as columns and a third tree as a beam connecting the two trees. Then she took some of the old wooden planks that once belonged to the gate and made rafters for the roof. On top of the rafters, she placed lots of jungle leaves, making the roof waterproof. She also stacked some cut-up wood against the wall, under the roof, to keep it dry for the fire at night.

"Flower, you have done a great job making this place livable. Your father and mother would be so proud of you if they could see this place and what you have done with it."

"John, are you okay? You are sweating a lot."

"Huh? Oh… It feels like I have a fever," he said, placing his hands to his forehead. He hadn't noticed, but now that she mentioned it, he did feel hot. He figured it was the fire. "My bullet wound is getting red; I hope it's not getting infected."

"Well, let's go to the little town I told you about earlier. I knew an old lady there once. She was a good friend of mine. I saw her as my grandmother. She took care of me often while growing up with my parents. Her name is Uma and, if she's still there, she can help you with medicine and clean up your wound real good. She can also help you with writing material, so that you can write to your wife and let her know that you are in good hands."

They both jumped up on Toby's back and began their journey to this little town. "I will let you see for yourself what this town has to offer. That way the journey there will be more pleasant. You can fill your mind with expectations of the unknown."

"Once again, well spoken words, Flower."

As the ride continued, John began to think about Flower and her wisdom at such young age. After all, doesn't wisdom comes from the things we have been through? Therefore, the saying, 'You grow wiser as you grow older,' seemed true in the presence of Flower. She was so young, but still spoke as a wise person. She'd had more to experience than a child her age should ever have to. But the fruit of that was wisdom. We are who we have in our life.

It was obvious that Flower's parents had done a great job teaching her about what was truly important: to make a difference in the lives of others by the way you live. By being an example of how to act toward people. They built a foundation in her life by having a relationship with God and living by His Word.

For His Word is all about love and how important it is for everyone to have love in their hearts in order to be truly happy.

If Flower didn't have the love of God in her heart, would she survive the wild jungle and its darkness every night?

John could imagine how much her faith must have grown in God, to trust in Him alone, while being in the jungle all this time, without having any human contact. He couldn't understand the strong affection and compassion he had for Flower, unless God had ordained them to be a new family together.

At that moment his thoughts were interrupted by Flower saying, "Look John, there is a tapir eating ants with his long tongue in the ant nest!" Flower knew a lot about the jungle and could name all the animals that crossed their path. While looking at the surroundings of the jungle, John heard what sounded like a roar further off. It gave him an uneasy feeling.

Flower was quick to answer his silent unease and said, "That's the sound of a wild tiger looking for something to eat. But don't worry, John, we are safe as long as we are sitting on Toby's back."

John felt tense at the thought of a wild tiger nearby, but was able to be at ease knowing that Toby was protecting them. His thoughts drifted toward his wife and how much she would enjoy this elephant ride. How much she would love Flower. John knew that she would love to adopt her and be able to care for her as her own daughter. So the unanswered question came to his mind again. "What are your plans for your future? I mean, after all the nice conversations we've shared with each other, about our lives and what we been through personally… You are a young girl and someone needs to take care of you and your future. It's also important that you finish schooling so you can earn a degree, so that when you become an adult you can get a job, earn an income, and be able to take care of yourself. I can help you with all this if you come with me to England to live with us. We can be a family together. Is it wrong of me, for the first time in a long time, to have a desire in my heart to really believe that we can do this together? My hope is still to give a child to my wife. To me, Flower, you are that child."

"I understand how you feel. I saved your life. I know the feeling of true love, when someone wants to give their life to someone else. You feel toward me like I feel toward Toby. When I saved Toby from being stuck in the hole, in reality, we saved each other from death. If I had never run into Toby, I would never have made it on my own in this jungle. Toby gave me the desire to want to carry on, when I wasn't sure I could.

"How can an elephant give you the desire to live, after all, he is just an animal? The answer is, because of love. When I felt that I had lost everyone I loved, my heart was crushed into so many pieces, that all I wanted to do was vanish, to die. How can you have the desire to live, if you don't have anyone who loves you?

"I tried to make Toby leave me. I was angry for what had happened to my parents. I shouted from the top of my lungs to Toby, 'Get out of here! Go back to your family; I am no good for you!' How could God take away all that I lived for, my loving parents? Then I fell down on my knees, feeling so empty and naked inside. My emotions overwhelmed me into a sadness I had never before felt in my life. So I wept and wept.

"After weeping and crying for a long time, I decided to open my eyes and see who was standing next to me. Surprisingly, it was Toby. I was sure that he'd left because I'd shouted at him to leave. For good. So believing that I was all alone in the jungle, knowing that I couldn't survive on my own, I began to cry in fear of losing my life. I didn't want to die alone. So you can imagine my happiness to see Toby beside me. From that moment on, Toby has never left my side.

"This last year with so much time to myself in the jungle, I began to think a different way, with depth, looking up to God. God says in the Bible, 'My thoughts are not your thoughts, neither are your ways my ways.' Would we have met the way we met if my parents were still alive? God gives and takes away. He opens new doors and closes old doors, but they all serve the same purpose. To make a new and better life for everyone who has love in their hearts. 'For there is no fear in love, but perfect love casts out fear. Because fear has to do with punishment, the one who fears is not made perfect in love.' The love between people is far from perfect, because no one is perfect, but God's love is.

"I remember when my father was still alive and how much I loved to be with him. I loved him so much that I was scared to hurt him. I was scared to disappoint him, by messing up something and making him angry with me. Sure, he forgave me when I did something wrong, and would remind me of it by saying, 'How many times must I tell you that you are forgiven?' I know in my heart that as long as I do my best, God will do the rest. It's easier to love than to forgive, but you must learn to forgive in order to perfect your love.

"I was very upset with God, when my parents were taken away from me. I was not willing to accept what had happened, because I couldn't understand why it happened. I have learned to accept what I can't understand. Why would we need God if we understood everything? I know that life doesn't seem fair sometimes because of the circumstances and situations thrown at us that seem to have no meaning.

"A year ago, I could not, but today I can say with joy in my heart that my parents are with God. I asked God, 'Are my parents with You?' and He said, 'Yes.' I believe that God allows things to happen to us, things that we do not like, so we can learn to become more forgiving, and therefore more loving, in His likeness. Our mistakes also keep us humble, to remind us that we are not perfect."

"You lift me up so much when you speak about God. You speak with such understanding," John said to her.

"That's because I was taught to live for God at an early age. Every day I would read the Bible with my parents. Talking about God was a daily routine for our family. My dad used to say to me that in order to become a good servant of God, you need to store His Word in your heart. To do your best to present yourself to God as one approved, a workman that does not need to be ashamed and who correctly handles the Word of truth.

"With that said, I'm sorry to disappoint you, John, but I can't leave Toby here by himself and go with you to England."

"Oh Flower, I would never bring you to England without Toby coming with us. I'm sure that there won't be any problem for us to arrange something so Toby can come along. I am more concerned about how and when it can be possible for you to leave. I can't just put you on a plan and take you home. You and I both need a passport to leave this country legally. We need to go to the English Embassy to arrange paperwork regarding adopting you.

Hey, It looks like we're almost to our destination. I can see rooftops..."

"Yes John, you are looking at the town we are going to. It will still take us about fifteen minutes before we reach the town. I think I should fill you in about this town and the people living here. I'm sure you're curious to hear about it.

"My father had bought some land here and started his business to produce tea. When he started, he hired ten people to work for him. First they prepared the land. There was a lot of cleanup necessary to get this land ready for planting. My father removed all the trees and we used them to build our house. This little town has been built with body labor only, without machines. The times when excessive force was needed, people used elephants for help with the heavy work of removing.

"My father learned about several problems they have in India regarding floods.

So he bought a piece of land located on top of a hill and therefore did not have to worry about losing his house in a flood.

"Half of my father's life, he worked as a carpenter, since his father was also a carpenter and his grandfather as well. So of course this trade of carpentry became a tradition in his family. My father loved to build things out of wood, mostly houses. He told me that it is a great feeling to be able to drive around and say, 'I built all these houses.' My father told me that by coming and living among these poor people, he received the secret to having peace in his life. He said to me, "By having nothing you can see everything the way you should see it.'

"Having many things in this world makes it easier to want to have more things and you don't feel satisfied until you get it. Once you get it, you want something else and before you know it, you are stuck in an evil circle, where you will never be satisfied or able to feel contentment with what you have. You will always be chasing after more and this becomes a lifestyle.

"Many people in this world are chasing a lie that can never be found in the things of the world, but only by love can we make changes for a better future. My mother once told me that it was a hard choice to make, to leave England and all the things they had of the world.

"To be honest, my mother told me that my father and she experienced something they had never experienced until coming to India. My parents told me that by coming to India and this little town, they both tasted something very important that they had never tasted before, and that was the feeling of being surrounded by love wherever they looked.

"The people here didn't care what kind of clothes you wore, how you looked or what things you came with. They greeted my parents with such beautiful smiles. It made them feel like they had always belonged here. Once they tasted this love, it changed them for the better. This new love made them feel so alive and they wanted to become part of it. So, as my mother told me, our lives changed 180 degrees in a new direction and we started living by loving others first. It's so rewarding for your heart to help those in need, when you can. So my parents fell in love with these people and the way they treated them.

"All right John, I got little sidetracked, so let's go back

to the beginning again. My father had bought a chainsaw and began to clean the branches off the trees. He began building the house frame and the outer walls with tree logs. He cut them lengthwise, shaping and fitting the logs together as a puzzle. When the house was done, my father gave a party to the whole town with lots of good food, with recipes from England.

"At this time my parents hired a woman by the name of Uma, to help my parents prepare the food for the party. Her husband had died a year earlier by drowning. "My brother is actually an adopted child. My father's older brother and his wife got killed in a traffic accident and no one wanted to take care of Jack except my parents. Coming to India, Jack was four years-old and my parents wanted him to learn the native language here, so Uma got hired for that task as well. The bond between Uma and my parents grew strong. So when I was born, Uma was asked to become my nanny. She was delighted to be asked for such responsibility and said yes gladly.

"Uma is like a grandmother to me. My mother taught her how to speak English rather quickly, since my mother was a housewife and therefore they were able to spend lots of time together. In the beginning when my parents met Uma, she was rather bitter at heart due to losing her husband the way she did, by drowning. She was quick to complain about life and how she had lost everything she cared for.

"Knowing why Uma was so bitter gave my parents more patience with her attitude. They wouldn't give up on her troubled heart. My parents helped Uma to believe in herself again. Because my parents always loved her and encouraged her, Uma found again the desire in her heart to learn and become a more loving person. So Uma asked my parents, 'How can I become more loving like you?'

"My father showed the way and told Uma how with these words: 'You must have a relationship with Jesus, not because someone else tells you to, but because you want to. When you give your heart to Jesus and want to live for Him, His love can come into your heart and transform you into His likeness. You might wonder how you will know if you have received His love into your heart. You will know. You will not speak the way you used to speak, nor think the way you used to think or even feel the way you used to feel toward life and people. Your dreams and desires will all become new, and you will want to live to please God Himself, by loving people the way He loves us. You will begin to look at all people through His eyes, the potential in who they can be if they come to God and build a relationship with Jesus.'

"Last time I saw Uma she had a round face with a big smile and her hair was starting to turn greyish. She is short, chubby, and she is a very loving person."

Those were the last words Flower had time to share with John before they entered the town.

Restoring My Life

They continued their ride through the town while people stared at them like they had seen a ghost. John whispered softly into Flower's ear and said, "Why are they looking at us like they've never seen two people riding an elephant before?"

Before Flower had a chance to answer his question, she stopped Toby in his tracks and looked wide-eyed at an older woman standing in front of them. Flower's eyes connected with the woman's eyes and as they were looking at each other, the woman began to cry.

After a moment the woman said to Flower, "Get down from the elephant right now. I need to give you a hug."

Flower made her way off of Toby's back and onto the ground. With tears, they hugged each other. John could hear what the woman was saying, as she spoke with Flower.

"Thank you God, that she is still alive and thank you, Lord for listening to my prayers."

Flower replied to Uma, "Look at you! You have become so skinny since the last time I saw you. I hope you are not sick!"

Uma answered back, "The sickness is called worry.

Everyone believed you were killed in the fire along with your parents. The police who came to investigate the death of your parents only found their remains. After three months, the whole town lost hope of seeing you again, but not me. Something spoke to my heart that you were still alive. I didn't know the truth regarding what happened to you. I began to worry about you and your well-being, where you could be, and that made me depressed and lose my appetite."

The people of the town wanted to give Flower a hug and make sure they were not looking at a ghost.

Uma turned to John and said, "Whoever you are, I want to thank you for bringing Florence back to me."

"My name is John Campbell. It's a long story. And I didn't bring Florence to you... she brought me to you."

Uma then looked at Florence and said to her, "You could've come home all this time? And none of us, especially me, had to worry about you all this time? I don't understand why you would bring so much pain to us by staying away and not coming back home," she said.

Florence answered Uma, "Like John said, it's a long story. Let's go up to my father's guesthouse and there we can share information with each other, between the three of us."

So after all the hugging was done, they left the crowd and began to walk toward the guesthouse.

All the way up, Florence and Uma held hands and shared tears of joy for being back together again. When they arrived at the guesthouse, Uma and Florence went inside, while Toby and John took a moment to enjoy the beautiful scenery surrounding them.

First, John looked down toward the town in the valley. All of the buildings, apartments, and houses were built one-story high. All apartments had a roof overhang in the front of the building. The people of the town could sit under a roof and still socialize while it was raining. The rain season often lasted for months there.

Beyond the town John could see fields of tea getting ready for harvest. Then John observed the guesthouse and behind it, a beautiful garden. Well, it could have been beautiful. A lack of maintenance made it overgrown with weeds. The garden was in need of a serious cleanup so its beauty could be revealed again.

Beyond the garden was the edge of the jungle with all its trees and tight vegetation. You could hear birds singing and monkeys howling. Then another voice was heard, the voice of Uma shouting to John, "Come inside and join me and Florence for a cup of tea!"

John walked inside to join their company and said to Florence, "This guesthouse is rather big. It has a second floor?"

"My father had it built big, so if anyone came to visit us, they could stay as long as they needed in the guesthouse. You can see the first floor has a kitchen, living room and bedroom. The door you see in the corner is not a closet, but leads to a bathroom with a shower and a toilet. Upstairs are two more bedrooms with closets."

Then Uma cut in into the conversation and said, "While you were outside, Florence shared with me information regarding how you both met and what you have been through. Let me look at your bullet wound." John opened his shirt for her examination. Uma began to look at his wound and said to Florence, "I'm glad that you brought him here as soon as possible. He definitely has an infection and needs antibiotics. Luckily, we have a doctor who is coming tomorrow to see someone else who is sick. He will be here first thing in the morning."

John said to Uma, "I have given Florence a nickname, Flower, because I have seen the amazing gift this girl has been given when it comes to arranging flowers."

Uma answered back, "I like the name you have given her. She's a very special girl just like her parents were. Knowing that they were Christians and seeing the way they loved me, put me to shame and I wanted to be able to love the way they loved and cared for people. So one day I asked Flower's father, Simon, the most important question of my life. How can I begin to have a relationship with God?

"Simon explained to me how to enter a relationship with Jesus, God's Son. Through Him you must be born again. He gave me a Bible and began to teach me about God and how much He loves us all. Simon told me that we are spiritual beings. That we need to feed ourselves spiritually as well as physically. In order for us to be truly loving, we need to feed ourselves from the Bible, which is full of God's love.

"Simon taught me to never force anyone to God, but to be patient. Be a good living example for people around you to see God's strength in you, by always loving everyone. Then you encourage them by speaking in love, by helping them see that there is still hope for better. Simon showed me the way to receive salvation, which means deliverance from guilt coming from sin.

"Today I have a new heart that God has given me for coming to Him. God's love in my heart humbles me. My outlook on life today is that I have been blessed to share many happy days together with my loving husband and I enjoy looking back on the beautiful love we once had. I also understand that this is the biggest blessing in life. It is important for us all to have someone to love and to love us back, to have someone to miss and to share dreams with, someone who wants to listen and help you with your struggles, and someone who is always faithful and by your side.

"Especially having someone who is quick to forgive you, for things you've done wrong, knowing that no one is perfect. And who once has forgiven you, never brings up the past again. I must speak the truth. No one else but God alone can give you all this. If you allow Him into your heart, you can have all of the qualities that you are searching to find in a relationship. The best quality is this: God will never leave you nor forsake you.

"Isn't fear our worst enemy in a human relationship? Fear that the one you love will leave you because you made a mistake and they won't forgive you? Or the fear in your heart when you ask yourself questions like, 'What if I get cancer? Will he be by my side to the end?' The list of fear in our lives can go on and on. So yes, fear of the unknown is the worst enemy of our lives, if we allow fear to control us.

"We want to have answers, even when we can't provide one. You want to see a miracle? Look at me and how God changed my lonely life and made it richer with His love in my heart.

What about this big miracle of God? "There once was an alcoholic and drug addict. Because of never being spiritually sober he was led to do even more bad things, like lusting sexually, committing burglary and stealing to provide for his drug habit. He became a disgrace to his parents and they wanted nothing to do with their son anymore. He found himself in the bottom of the barrel with a crushed heart and a broken spirit thinking, 'How did I end up like this?' He didn't recognize himself anymore and he ended up hurting everyone who was close to him.

"He had gone too far and felt that there was no way out of his lifestyle, no way to make things right again. With a broken heart, he thought to himself, 'I may as well take my life.' At that moment he began to cry thinking, 'I wish I had another chance to be a good son.' The Bible says, 'The Lord is close to the brokenhearted and saves those who are crushed in spirit.'

"So God's grace was poured on this man to help him ask God for help. Having nothing left of himself, this man called out to God with a sincere heart with these words. 'God, I need your help. I can't take this pain any longer in my heart. If you help me out of this mess and take my pain, I will live for you.'

"The next day at sunrise this man went to a park and sat down on a bench to admire the beautiful morning of a new day. He felt different. While sitting on the bench, a man came and sat down next to him. This man was not an ordinary man. He was an angel sent from God. The angel, looking like a man, didn't waste any time approaching the man with a broken heart.

"The angel asked the man how he was doing. No

one had asked him this question for so long. It made him feel so loved, which he had been longing for as long as he could remember. He began to cry. Then the angel asked him, 'Are you okay?' He answered the angel, 'No, everyone hates me and wants nothing to do with me anymore.'

"The angel looks into the man's eyes and said, 'There is someone who loves you right now. His name is Jesus. He can take away all your pain, give you a new heart and make you into a new man. All you have to do is accept Him as your Lord and Savior and believe that God raised Him back from death and His love will come into your heart right now.' Having nothing to lose but his life, the man with the broken heart willingly accepted the terms to let Jesus come into his heart, by asking for forgiveness for all the sins he had done.

"At that very moment, God changed this man forever. It felt like a weight had disappeared in his heart and the burden he used to have, was gone just like that. However, the man was gone and he realized that God had answered his cry for help. Not knowing where to go for help or how to get on his own feet again, he decided to go to his old church, where he used to attend many years before.

"The old priest remembered him and helped him find housing and food. The priest also helped him with a job. He joined a Bible study group at church and attended every sermon the pastor had at the church. The hunger and desire to serve God was so strong in this man's heart that he went to a Bible school to study and become a pastor. After finishing school and having a talent to speak and express himself regarding God's love for all of us, a door opened for him. The pastor asked him to preach the Word of God in his church.

"He felt led in his heart to preach about forgiveness. So, who came to church that Sunday? His family who wanted nothing to do with him anymore. Many of his old friends also showed up. The first thing he said while looking at his parents was, 'I didn't know that God is all I need, until God was the only thing I had left in my life.'

"Before he began to preach about forgiveness, he shared his testimony with everyone in the church. He shared about who he once was, who he became and what God took him out of and made him into. His parents began to cry along with his old friends. Many people in the church were crying as well.

"How can this not be a beautiful miracle? Everyone who knew who he once was and how he used to live, were now watching a new man preaching about God's perfect love. Think about how long this miracle will stay alive in their hearts, in the hearts of those who remember him the way he used to be and today can see with their own eyes, what God has done for this man.

"Today his relationship with his family is completely restored. Isn't it a beautiful story? It brought tears to my eyes the first time Simon told me this story. Simon told me that it put his heart to shame, for giving up on his younger brother, after seeing what God had done for him. His brother is the man from the story.

"This miracle from God, made Simon and his wife's faith stronger than ever. So because of this wonderful family, I have been given another chance to live a richer life than ever, because of Christ's sacrifice for me. I never felt like having a child until I met my husband. We met when we were in our fifties, so I was too old to become pregnant.

"But enough about me, let us talk about Flower and her future. You don't know about this Flower, but your father arranged through a lawyer, a will for you and your brother and all of the necessary paperwork regarding his business, in case the unforeseen should happen. Your father also gave me a phone number to call your brother Jack if something like this should happen.

"Since I didn't know if you were alive or not, I haven't called him yet. He sent a letter addressed to your parents last week. Since they are gone, I took the freedom to open the letter and read it myself.

"Jack is doing well and will be done with his tour before Christmas and he said he can't wait to come home and spend time with his family again."

Uma then looked at John and asked "What about you, John, what are your plans from here?"

"Well, I can understand why Simon and his wife fell in love with this place and wanted to move here. I don't believe that they moved here for business alone, but for the warmth of love and caring of these people. I have never been here before, but already it feels like I have belonged to this place and its people for a long time. The first thing on my list is to write to my wife and let her know that I am well and have found a great place with great people and that I would love for her to come here so we can spend Christmas together."

"Yes John, you need to write a letter to your wife right

away, so when the doctor leaves tomorrow, he can take the letter with him and have it posted immediately."

Flower cut in and asked Uma, "What about my father and his business?"

"The people of the town kept the business going by planting a new crop, which is ready in two weeks for harvest. But by the lack of money and resources, it looks like Simon's business will end if no one comes to rescue it."

"Wait a minute," John replied, "These people will not suffer a loss as long as I'm here. I am a wealthy man and I will provide whatever these people need to get the harvest done and to keep the business going. After all, I'm alive because Flower found me and saved me from death."

Uma replied, "Tomorrow I will call the family lawyer to meet with us and discuss the future of Simon's business."

"What do you have to say, Uma, regarding the garden and why it looks like it does? I don't like being so close to the jungle alone, because I don't feel safe. I hope the three of us can live together in the guesthouse and have Toby on the outside. He makes me feel safe. Then we can be a family again," said Flower.

"As you can see Flower, I have been keeping the guesthouse clean. Once in awhile I brought someone with me to help clean and maintain the inside of the guesthouse. In hope for your return, I kept it clean."

Flower said, "Well it's about two hours before sunset. I would like to spend some time with Toby alone. He and I are going for a ride in the jungle."

"Will you be okay in the jungle by yourself?" asked Uma.

"You are so sweet Uma. You have always looked out

for my best interest and safety. I will be okay, remember that Toby and I has been living in the jungle for almost a year. It will also give you and John some quality time to get to know each other better."

"Promise me, Flower, that you will be back before the sun is down. I will have dinner ready by the time you're back. Please be careful in the jungle."

"I will Uma. I promise nothing will happen to me, because Toby will be by my side. Just enjoy the time together with John while I am gone. He is a very nice man and I know that you will like him."

With that said, Flower left with Toby and Uma and John began a nice conversation about Flower. John started the conversation by saying, "Do you remember how quickly Flower changed the subject when you asked her why she had been gone all this time and made you all suffer for it? It's obvious that you don't know the truth about Flower's parents and how they died. Two men shot them to death. Then the men dragged their bodies inside the house and set it on fire."

When Uma heard this, it made her very upset and troubled, and she said to John, "When Flower comes back, like it or not, she must make a statement and describe how these two men looked. The doctor can take this statement with him and give it to the police, so they can make a warrant for these evil men and justice can be done.

"They need to pay for taking Simon´s and Sheryl's lives and making Flower parentless. I am so sorry to interrupt you John, as you were telling me about Flower. Remember, when she comes back from the jungle, her statement must be done right away."

"I will make sure that it is done before she goes to bed, I promise you that Uma."

"Thank you so much. She means the world to me. Go ahead and continue your story about Flower."

"Okay, where was I with my story?"

"The two men were setting the house on fire."

"That's right; thank you for reminding me. Flower witnessed all this from the edge of the jungle by her parents' house. Fearing that the two men noticed her, she began to run for her life. She found Toby, who was stuck in a hole filled with muck and couldn't escape its grip. After Flower helped Toby out of the hole, they both left together going into the jungle and haven't been apart since.

"I was also running, fearing for my life. While lying on the jungle floor, I looked up to the sky and thought I heard the enemy coming toward me from the jungle to take my life. Instead, my life was granted to continue through Flower and Toby, by their coming and rescuing me.

"She took care of my wound with herbs and stopped the bleeding. Then she took me to the place where they had been living. This place is an old abandoned temple, a temple that was destroyed a long time ago, but through the hands of Flower and the strength of Toby, it was made into a dream place. You must see it one day."

"My heart goes out to you completely, John," said Uma, "I understand the pain and I have been through the same experience, in a different way, when my husband passed away. It's a terrible feeling to not be able to give a child to the one you love and have a family together. My husband and I fell in love for the first time at an old age.

We both wished that our love for each other could have happened at an earlier age, to have a child and our own family together. Instead, God gave me Flower to look after and to love as my own child.

"Flower also told me that you would love to adopt her and start a family together with your wife. As long as Flower is okay with it, you have my blessing to make it happen. I promise you this, I will personally see to it that all of the paperwork is done in order for you and your wife to adopt Flower and to continue the good work of raising her where her parents left off.

"Right now I think you should rest and take a nap until dinner is ready. I will go down and get some vegetables, rice, and fresh fish of the day. I will be right back to cook the dinner for tonight."

"Thank you, Uma, that sounds very nice." When Uma left John, he closed his eyes and fell asleep very quickly.

When Uma went back to the town, the people saw her going into her tiny apartment. Quickly the town spokesman knocked on her door to talk about what the town could do for Florence. The name of the spokesman was Joshi and his first words to Uma were, "We would like to build a new home for Florence where the old one once stood."

Excited and liking the surprise a lot, Uma opened the door and said out loud to the people of the town, "That is a great and excellent idea! We all know what Florence's parents have done for many of us and for this town. They taught us how to live and work in unity, by loving and caring for each other. Florence's parents taught us to forgive each other, to forget the former things and to not dwell in the past. You all make me very proud, to see your love spoken in action to Florence who needs our support right now."

Uma told the townspeople, "Florence has been through a lot this last year because she witnessed her parents being killed, when we thought it was an accident. Not knowing if the murderous men saw her or not, she hid all this time, along with an elephant that she found in the jungle. Her fear of coming back here and being noticed by the men who killed her parents, is the reason why we haven't seen her until now.

"I can tell that the year she has spent on her own in the jungle has really matured her beyond her age. Promise me one thing, people, since you know the truth about Florence's parents and their death. Don't talk about her parents' death in front of her."

The people of the town and Uma all came to an agreement to make Florence happy again, whatever it took. The people left with big smiles on their faces and excitement about the surprise for Florence in the morning. Uma was quick to collect the food in her apartment and rushed back to the guesthouse to share the great news with John.

When Uma came back to the guesthouse, John was still asleep. Uma came up to him and with her soft voice, whispered into his ear to wake him up and tell the news. "When I went down to my place, the people of the town came and shared a surprise with me, that I must share with you before Flower comes back home. Tomorrow morning when Flower wakes up, the whole town will be standing outside the guesthouse to tell her that they are going to build a new house for her where the old one used to be. I'm so sorry that I woke you up from your nap, but I just couldn't wait until tomorrow for you to find out. I just had to share the surprise with you right now, so we both can look at Flower's face and see her reaction when she hears her surprise. Go ahead and continue your nap while I cook dinner for us."

Meanwhile, Flower and Toby enjoyed being together in the jungle like they used to be. Flower stood next to Toby and talked to him. Looking into his eyes, her heart filled with gratitude. Flower kneeled down on the ground and began to pray to God, "Father God, I want to thank you for taking away the loneliness from my heart, by bringing John into my life. By doing so, the void of missing my father has been filled in my heart. Father God, I really like John a lot, please don't take him away from me. It would make me very happy if you could help them to be my new parents, so please Father God, let us become a family together. I miss so much having my own family. Thank you, God, for the wonderful relationship You have blessed me to have with You." Flower smiled and looked up at Toby. "What do you say Toby? I guess we better get home for a nice dinner."

Uma and John met them outside. Uma greeted them by saying, "Perfect timing! I just finished cooking dinner for us." In Uma's hand was a big bowl of mixed fruit for Toby to eat. So Toby began to eat his fruit outside and they went inside to enjoy a tasty dinner. The dinner was breaded fish with rice and a spicy sauce along with a nice salad. They all enjoyed this lovely dinner together, being in a family once again.

After dinner, Uma suggested that they would go outside and watch the sun set over the town, from the top of the hill. Leaving a satisfying sense of taste they went outside to enjoy the sense of sight.

Flower said, "Wow, I've forgotten how beautiful the sunset is to watch from here."

John replied, "It sure is beautiful. I'm happy to be here watching it with all of us together."

Daylight was almost gone when they went back into the guesthouse to spend the night. Uma opened the conversation, "Flower, you must make a statement regarding how the two men looked, the men who killed your parents."

"I don't want to talk about it."

Uma was quick to answer back and said, "Flower, we must do our share to help to get these men behind bars. You don't want someone else to lose their parents, do you Flower? Believe me when I say, if they have done this to your parents, they can do it to someone else's as well."

"You are right Uma. We need to do what we can to bring these men to justice. Do you have a pen and a paper so I can describe the looks of these two men?"

"Yes I do, here is a pen and a paper. When you are done Flower, put it on the kitchen table and I will make sure it will go tomorrow with the doctor. When he gets back to the big city, he can hand it over to the police, and they can make a warrant for their arrest."

Flower began to write a statement of how the two men looked.

And John began to write a letter to his wife.

A Letter of Forgiveness

Dear Sarah,

My wish is that this letter will find you well and that it will bring hope to your heart.

I know that no words can replace the pain I have put you through, by me being here and you wondering if I am well.

All I can say is, I am so sorry and please forgive me. Please read this letter with an open heart. I hope for our love to grow again.

Something most amazing happened to me a few days ago, when I thought that God had closed the door on my life and I was left to die in a jungle of India. I was shot in the chest while running away from gunfire, from an attack on the village, and a miracle happened.

As I was lying on my back on the jungle floor with no strength left, I heard something coming toward me, and thought it must be the enemy to come and finish me off.

To my surprise, it was a little girl riding on an elephant, and they saved me.

The elephant's name is Toby. He picked me up and placed me on his back and together with the girl, we rode into the jungle for safety. We lost the men chasing after me.

The girl, Florence, took me to an abandoned temple where she and the elephant had been living for almost a year on their own. Two men who came to rob them killed Florence's parents at their house. Florence witnessed her parents being murdered from the edge of the jungle. She saw it right in front of her own eyes. Florence feared that these two men had seen her and would want to take her life as well. In her fear, she ran into the jungle where she met Toby. She saved him from dying. He was stuck in a hole of muck and couldn't get out. At that moment, they became friends and have been together as one since.

Because of an infection in my bullet wound and a need for medicine, Florence found the courage to go back to the town with me. She felt better knowing that I would be by her side to protect her from those two men.

When we came to the town, the townspeople greeted us with such warm love, that I fell in love with these people and their beautiful little town.

I cannot describe the strong desire and hope for a better future together, you and I, with this girl in our lives. I want to adopt her to be our daughter, so that together we can take care of her. I hope to build up a family together, which we for so long have been desperate to have.

My wish for us is that you can come here for Christmas and meet Florence and Toby and all these other loving people.

I would like you to prepare all the paperwork in England regarding adoption, and bring them with you. I will not leave this place without Florence. I love this girl and I know that you will as well.

Being over here and feeling so alone made me seek God for company and to see if He could help to fill the emptiness in my heart. My relationship with God has grown so strong over here and I truly believe that God has opened a door for us, through Florence, to have a family together.

She is an amazing and strong girl. She claims that she never would have survived in the jungle without knowing that God was at her side and kept her safe.

Her parents were Christians and I can tell that they were strong believers by the way Florence speaks about how great our God is. He made it possible for her to live in the jungle all this time, without having fear of the jungle's darkness and its wild animals. Sarah, you have always had strong faith in God and you always tried to make me see the importance of reading the Bible together and therefore, to stay in the light of life.

I want to say that I am sorry for not listening to you regarding the importance of having a relationship with God. To be honest, back then, I didn't understand what I understand today. That the word light means love.

I have also learned that human love and God's love are different. When you find God's love in your heart, you begin to live and love in a way you never have before. And that makes you feel special.

Back home in England, before coming here, I was nothing but selfish. All I cared about was myself and looking good for the world. I didn't listen to you Sarah. I had no time for God. I have found something different in my heart and I love it. It makes me forget about myself and all I want to do is to reach out and help those in need.

I'm talking about God's love in my heart. We cannot love the way God desires for us to love, because of the sin in us. I understand today that God sent His Son Jesus into the world as a light, which stands for love. Only love can make this world a better and friendlier place.

For God did not send His Son into the world to condemn the world, but to save the world through Him, by His love being found in our hearts. Without light nothing living can grow healthy. When I found God's love in my heart, I became troubled by the pain you must have been through because of my actions.

Believe me, Sarah, when I say that I am not the same man who left you. I hope that you are willing to give our love a new chance, by giving me a new chance as a new man with a strong faith in God.

So take care, Sarah, I am waiting for our love to begin to grow together again as one in God. Come soon.

With love, sincerely,
Your husband

To Care for One Another

As Uma watched Flower and John write letters, she decided that she should write a letter to Flower's brother, Jack, and let him know the situation regarding his parents' death. He should know who was taking care of his sister.

Uma thought that it would be easier for Jack to deal with the news of his parents' over there, rather than hearing the first of it at home when he came for Christmas.

So while Uma wrote a letter to Jack, Flower and John finished their letters and fell asleep, exhausted after an exciting day together.

The next morning at sunrise, all three of them woke up to someone knocking on the front door. Uma was the first one to go and see who it was. Acting surprised, she looked and said, "The whole town is outside and would like to speak to you, Florence."

Flower and John joined Uma outside to find out what the people wanted to say to Flower. A man standing in front of the crowd began to speak to Flower, "Good morning, Florence. My name is Joshi and I have been elected to speak on behalf of the people in this town. First, I want you to know how troubled we are regarding what happened to your parents, Simon and Sheryl. When they first came here fifteen years ago we didn't think much of them, but as time went by, they changed this town. We became more loving, kind, and helpful by the good example they set for all of us. They taught us to live in love by living in love themselves and therefore, we were able to learn to care for one another. We learned that anything is possible, if we all work together.

"I will never forget when I lost my whole crop one year because of a flood. Your father, Simon, heard about it and came to see me personally without my asking for his help. Simon said, 'I'm so sorry for what has happened to you, for it could happen to me as well. Let me help you financially until you sell next year's crop and then you can pay me back.'

"At that time I was living in a different town, where I was producing my own crop for a living. It felt like I was blessed with a miracle out of nowhere because of your father's quick response to help me. The flood happened in the morning and your father found out about me, and came to my rescue the same day in the afternoon. The following year I paid back all the money your father had loaned me in advance.

"That act of kindness changed my life. I became a more loving and caring person. The most amazing thing was that your father didn't know me and I didn't know him, but he still didn't hesitate to help me. That act of kindness made me want to work for him, so I asked him if I could come and work for him. Simon hired me as a foreman, because of my experience."

After Joshi shared these words of his personal testimony, another voice from the crowd cut in and said, "Florence, my name is Nana, and I would like to share with you what your mother did for me and my husband. Just like Joshi said, your parents really changed this whole town's attitude, by the way they lived and shared openly, modeling how we all should be toward one another.

"When they first came here, this town was not the same as it is today. We were all selfish and only thought of ourselves. Being poor and not having much, we still managed to be so proud. We did not want to show anyone that we were in need of help. Because of pride, we almost lost our only child, our daughter, to pneumonia. The medication for it was expensive and we didn't have enough money to pay for it. Our pride held us back from reaching out for help.

"If it wasn't for your mother who walked by our apartment and heard our daughter coughing, she would most likely be dead today because of a lack of medication. Your mother, Sheryl, stopped and asked me, 'What is wrong with your daughter? Why is she coughing so hard?' I told her that the cough was from pneumonia.

"Sheryl said to me, 'Don't you have medication for her?' I felt ashamed to tell her that I couldn't afford to buy the medication. I was about to feel even more ashamed than ever. She began to call out to everyone, 'Come here right now everyone! I must speak to you all.' After everyone had approached your mother, to hear what she had to say, she began to say angrily, 'How is it that this little girl has been sick for days and no one has cared to help? What if it was your own daughter? Would you be so selfish, that you wouldn't ask for help as well? You are telling me that you are willing to let this girl die just because you don't care? Or is it because you think that no one would help you, if you were in the same situation? The truth is, it's not about you, but right now you are holding this little girl's life in your hands. All you have to do is come together and give a small donation, and this girl's life can continue to be part of your lives. Please, who can help, with a little donation, to make her healthy?' This was the only time I saw your mother become angry on some else's behalf.

"I have never seen people so quick to give a donation to help someone in need as after your mother spoke to the crowd."

Joshi then said to Florence, "These stories have one thing in common. We can all make an impact on one another, for better or worse, depending on how one reacts in situations among people. With every action comes a reaction, which leads to a consequence. Your parents always reacted with love, and that changed us all to be more loving and caring for one another.

"Your parents taught us all that a man is not what he has, but rather what he is willing to give out of his own heart. Love does not give up, but is always quick to encourage, because there is always hope in love. For love does not quit on us, but we are quick to give up on love. Your parents taught us all that love can be received for free, if you are willing to freely give it. So Florence, we all come together this morning to give honor to your parents for how they made an impact for the better on this town and its people.

"We would freely like to give back to you what your

parents gave us. We desire to build a new house for you. What do you say, Florence? Would you like to have your house back?"

With tears running down her cheeks, Florence was speechless. She nodded yes to the crowd and in that very moment everyone clapped their hands to honor Florence's parents. Full of emotion from missing her parents so much, she began to weep and ran into the guesthouse.

Uma and John both knew that she needed some time on her own to process all of this. As people returned to their homes, Uma and John shook everyone's hands and thanked them all for their kindness and love for wanting to do this for Florence.

After they were all gone, Uma and John sat down on a bench and continued to enjoy the moment of happiness. About half an hour later Uma said to him, "You must be starving, would you like to have some breakfast?"

John replied, "I would love to."

After Flower pulled herself together, she joined them for breakfast in the kitchen. They were almost done eating breakfast when someone knocked on the door. Uma opened the door to find the doctor who had come to look at John's wound.

"Hello," he said, "I am Doctor Kumar. Joshi asked if I would come and examine John after my previous appointment." He came inside and began to examine John's bullet wound. The result of the examination was that he needed to go with the doctor to his clinic. John asked the doctor, "Is it okay if I bring Flower with me?"

Doctor Kumar looked at Flower and said, "I think it would be best if you came along."

Knowing that she couldn't take Toby along with her, she asked Uma, "Can you watch over Toby while we are gone?"

"Of course I will take care of Toby, don't you worry about a thing. Make sure that you help John with all the things he needs to take care of."

"Yes Uma, I will do that."

Then Flower, the doctor, and John left together.

Quality Time in the Big City

The journey began and Doctor Kumar asked John, "Do you have a passport with you?"

John answered, "No, all of my papers got lost in the incident at the border."

Doctor Kumar told him, "You need to go to the English Embassy to get a new passport. Luckily, the embassy was located in the city where the doctor lived.

Meanwhile, back at home the townspeople had already begun to build Flower's new home. They removed all of the debris from the old house and cleaned up the place where the old house used to stand. They began to build a new log home by cutting down some of the trees of the jungle from land, which belonged to Flower's parents. They used Toby to drag the trees, which they then made into logs to be used for the new house.

They all worked hard until sunset. The next day they got up early to continue building and were determined to finish her house before Flower and John returned. The men did the heavy work of constructing the house. Uma took charge of the cleanup and renewal of the garden. She wanted everything to look as it used to be, when Flower's parents still were alive.

Flower and John, along with Doctor Kumar, reached the big city.

First on the to-do list was to go to Doctor Kumar's clinic and take care of John's health. While Doctor Kumar was taking care of John's bullet wound, he said, "I feel it would be best for your health if you could stay here, for two nights anyway, so that I can give you a shot to help your healing and so your infection doesn't keep spreading while the antibiotics start to work." John agreed with the doctor's instruction and asked him for a favor.

"I would like to surprise Flower with a nice hotel with a pool. I'm not sure, but I think that she has never been swimming in a pool. She saved my life and it would be nice to do something special for this little girl. Can you arrange and pay for a hotel for us while we rest here? I'm a wealthy man, but there is one problem. All of my money is tied down in a bank account in England. I will not be able to pay you back until I get my passport and am able to transfer money from England to here. Can you please trust me, that I will pay you back?"

"John, because I know the family Anderson so well, I will help you with your request." After the examination and their conversation, Doctor Kumar treated Flower and John to lunch in a restaurant that was owned by a friend of the doctor.

After lunch they all went to the English Embassy so that John could apply for a new passport for himself and

Flower. Uma had already provided the documents for Flower to get a passport and had given them to John the night before. Uma also gave him the phone number of the family lawyer in case he had any trouble getting Flower a passport.

The embassy told John that he could come back for his and Flower's passports in two weeks. Two weeks was the day before Christmas Eve. While Flower and John were inside the embassy, Doctor Kumar was outside making phone calls to arrange for a hotel with a pool for them. John approached the doctor with expectation, hoping to hear some good news from him about a hotel.

Doctor Kumar said, "I have arranged everything you asked for and also paid for everything up front." Then the doctor gave John a paper with the address to the hotel and also wrote down his phone number in case of an emergency. "Tomorrow at one in the afternoon, go to the reception of your hotel. I have arranged a surprise for both of you. Oh… I almost forgot John; here is some spending money for you and Flower. There are some nice museums in the city, which I know you both would enjoy seeing." He continued, "Here John, give this note to the cab driver and he will take you to the hotel. I am sorry, but I have to leave and go back to work. I will see you in two days. Goodbye."

Doctor Kumar left, and Flower and John were left to face the big crowds of people in the big city. John was excited like a child to make this surprise happen for Flower. He asked her, "Have you been here before?"

Flower replied, "I've thought of visiting this city, but

I've never been here before. I must say that I am very excited to experience this city for the first time."

They crossed the street full of people and entered a taxi that was parked on the street. The taxi driver told them that it would take about half an hour to arrive at their destination. They sat in the taxi and watched people and the scenery of the city. John began to reflect on his life and people that he had met while being on the other side of the world.

As the ride continued, so did his thoughts. How could life and people be so different? How they lived and what they lived for and what kept them from not quitting, when they had nothing in the world to live for. That used to be his way of thinking before coming. He now saw and understood that life was more than the things one has.

In that moment he was taken out of a deep trance of thoughts, when Flower shouted, "Look John, I think we've arrived at our hotel."

The taxi driver confirmed Flower's guess by saying, "Yep, this is your hotel."

The hotel was painted in two colors. The walls were blue and the trim and borders were white. They stepped out of the taxi and paid for the trip. The taxi left and they looked around for a moment. Flower looked up toward the sky and the hotel's roof and said, "Wow... I have never seen such a tall building. It looks like it is going into heaven, it's so high up."

The hotel doorman approached them and interrupted by saying, "Welcome to Hotel Savarna."

With a big smile on his face, the doorman led them into the hotel. A woman behind the reception desk gave them information regarding the rules and regulations of the hotel. The first thing she said was, "I have been told that your stay here has been arranged as a surprise for both of you to enjoy during your time here. There is breakfast, lunch and dinner to be served here at the hotel, and has already been paid for. The first surprise will be tomorrow at one o'clock in the afternoon. You will get information from this desk. On the day you leave you must check out no later than twelve o'clock. Here is the key to your room. I will take you there personally. Let's go and see your room." As they walked to the elevator, the lady told them, "This hotel is twelve stories high."

They entered the elevator and she pushed the button for the twelfth floor. The woman left them by the door. When John opened the door, Flower ran inside to see what it had to offer. To their surprise, it wasn't an ordinary room. It was the penthouse.

The first thing they saw from the entryway foyer, looking into the living room, was a big beautiful glass bowl full of fruit. It was located on top of the living room table, which was made out of mahogany and was a display of beautiful craftsmanship. Around the rectangular table were leather couches to sit upon while enjoying the spectacular view.

All the exterior walls were dressed with big sliding doors made out of glass, so you could look outside in all four directions.

The penthouse also had a kitchen that was fully equipped. It had two bedrooms with their own bathrooms.

As John continued to look around, Flower shouted to him, "John come here! This must be my room! Look what's laying on the bed, a dress with an envelope with my name on it."

He walked into Flower's bedroom and said, "Go ahead and open the letter. It's addressed to you."

Flower opened the letter and read it. "As you can see, you are getting special treatment because you are a special to me. You will find everything you need to get cleaned up, to get dressed, and to look your best for your dinner tonight. There are also some casual clothes provided for you in the closet. Get yourself ready for dinner, which will be served at 7:00 pm at the Star Restaurant across the street from your hotel."

Excited, John ran into his bedroom to see if anything had been provided for him. On his bed were a white suit and a letter. Being curious about what the letter said, he opened and read it.

> Thank you John, for being so loving and caring to Florence. Just by watching you I can tell that you are both fond of each other. Remember when you asked me for the favor of giving Florence a surprise? This favor was already done in my heart before you even asked for it. I want you to understand something, John. Florence means the world to me. I have been her family doctor since she was born. I have seen this girl grow up and witnessed how special she is to everyone around her.
>
> She is a light because she is always full of life and shares her love with anyone, and she does it simply by always having a beautiful smile. It

would destroy my heart to see this light in her die out.

John, you are a blessing from above, for I know in my heart that you can help this light of Florence to continue to be a bright light to all people. All children need two things while growing up. They need someone to look up to and they need someone to love. You give her both and I believe that God blessed Florence with you coming into her life to be like a father to her.

So once again John, thank you. I want you and Florence to really enjoy your time together.

Sincerely,
Dr. Kumar

Touched, tears streamed down his face. Meeting Flower in the jungle truly changed his life's direction for the better. From feeling more and more empty inside and from lacking the feeling of being loved by people, his heart was now totally overflowing with the love of people all around him. He couldn't remember if he'd ever felt so alive and happy as he felt right then.

The funny thing is that he felt this way among people that he really didn't know. Perhaps it's because people there didn't judge you by what you had, but rather for who you were. It felt like he'd entered a dream and he didn't want it to end.

He dropped the letter on the bed and went in to his bathroom. On the countertop of the bathroom vanity was everything he could possibly need to shave and get cleaned up in the shower. After shaving, John jumped into the shower. He began to think about his wife and how much he truly missed her.

Meanwhile in the other bathroom, Flower had finished showering and was brushing her hair. She put on the light blue dress, which was made out of silk. Even her underwear was made out of silk. Flower loved the smooth feeling. She had never been dressed in silk before.

When John finished his shower, he dressed in a white shirt with a light blue tie, along with his white suit. He also put on his new shoes. Then from his bedroom, he went out onto the balcony to see the view. The balcony ran continuously around the penthouse floor. From there, the top of the building, you could enjoy the scenery in all directions.

As he stepped out onto the balcony, he found that Flower was already out there. Their eyes met over the distance between them. It was like the first time they had seen each other, because they looked so different, being cleaned up and wearing new clothes. John looked at Flower and felt amazed. Flower looked so beautiful in the dress she was wearing. She normally kept her long blond hair tied up, but now it hung freely below her waist.

With the sun setting behind her, the sunbeams seemed to light up her hair and make her look like an angel, complete with a beautiful smile, green eyes, red lips and round cheeks. Flower stared back at John, looking at his face, which was usually hiding behind a beard. She looked surprised to see him, too. "Wow, in that white suit I can really see what a tall and handsome man you are," she said. "And your tie makes the blue in your eyes so bright."

The clock showed them that it was ten minutes to seven, so they ran to the elevator, trying to be on time for their dinner. As they exited the hotel and walked to the restaurant, a young girl of about seven or eight years-old approached John and begged him to spare a coin for her.

He didn't give her a coin, but instead, he gave her a bill.

The girl sat down on her knees and with a bowed head, she said to John, "Thank you, you are so generous and kind. What you have given me will be food for me and my family for a few days."

They reached the door to the restaurant and walked inside. As soon as they went in, a woman greeted them by saying, "Welcome, I have been waiting and looking forward to serving you. Follow me and I will take you to your table."

She took them to a table at the back of the restaurant. Their table had beautiful flowers with two tall, lit candles. No other table in the restaurant was dressed as theirs, and it made them feel very special. The woman gave them a menu, took their drink order and said, "You can order whatever you want. It's already been paid in full. I will be back shortly with your drinks and to take your orders."

John turned his face toward Flower and said, "I don't know about you but I have felt like a king since we arrived at the hotel. Wherever we've gone, people have showered us with kindness."

Flower smiled and nodded, "Me too."

"Do you know what you want to order, Flower?"

"I have never seen any of these dishes before. I will let you order for me, John."

"I can do that for you. Just tell me what you like and don't like. Do you like fish?"

"Yes, I like fish."

"Let's do this, we'll order two different kinds of fish dishes and we can share to taste both of them."

"That's a good idea! So what are you going to order?"

"For you, Flower, I will order curry baked kingfish with fried rice and vegetables. And for me, I will order bread-crumbed whitefish, along with brown rice and vegetables. I think some garlic and herb sauce would taste good on the fish and rice. What do you think?"

"That sounds very good."

They received their fish dishes and shared them between the both of them.

It was a moment of good enjoyable fish, unlike any they'd ever tasted before. For dessert they enjoyed a banana split ice cream with peanuts. After finishing their nice dinner together, they decided to take a walk in the city. They didn't get very far from the restaurant when they were overwhelmed by lots of poor kids asking for money.

Since Flower and John were dressed so nicely and looked different from the people of the city, all the children flocked around them. They decided to go back to the hotel for the night. They were both tired after the trip and all the excitement of the day. Back at the hotel, John said, "Good night," and went to bed right away.

Flower was too excited to go to sleep.

Being around ten o'clock at night, she found herself in the kitchen looking for a snack, but nothing could be found to fill her taste for munchies. Then she spied the glass bowl full of fruit. It was located on the living room table. She walked up to the bowl and grabbed a banana from it.

Flower noticed a pen and a notepad lying on the table. She grabbed them and opened the sliding glass door in the living room and stepped out to look at the stars from the balcony. Her mind was full of thoughts and she felt led to write them down. She just needed to take a moment to compose herself.

She wondered at how the world could be so beautiful and ugly at the same time.

How could she feel so pretty, but also so ugly, when seeing all those poor children in the street? Could it be that for the first time in her life she felt helpless? She couldn't provide for all those children, not even what they needed the most: food.

Her heart was troubled after seeing the truth of poverty among the children. To see them and wonder how many more were out there living this life of begging for food and wondering if they would eat today. What a terrible feeling to have to wake up every morning and wonder if you would go to sleep hungry again that night. To wonder if you'd be lucky enough to find some leftover food somewhere.

Feeling sad, Flower began to cry from a heart full of gratitude for realizing how blessed she'd been growing up with her parents. She had a big blessing of freedom in her heart, to never have to worry about whether there would be food today or not.

Flower's heart had been full of dreams and desires, with the hope that she would find meaning and purpose in her life. This was another taste of the disappointment of not understanding why things were the way they were. With a troubled heart Flower looked up into the sky. The stars looked so dull compared to the sky at home. The city lights were reflected in the sky, making it harder to see the stars as good as back home where there were no streetlights. The city was busy, even at night, and quite loud. People shouted and cars beeped their horns, making it impossible for Flower to find the quietness that helped her fall asleep.

What a difference from being home. The night there was pitch black and you could see all the stars so clearly. You fell asleep by hearing nature singing to you, by its night creatures and insects.

Her father was right when he had told Flower that she wouldn't like the big city.

After sharing her troubled heart with God, she felt better and was ready to go to sleep. Flower put on her new pajamas and went to bed.

Being a new day and sleeping late into the morning, John was the first one to wake up. He lay in bed awake, looking out through the window. The sky made him remember a dream he'd had that night. Since Flower was in the dream, he felt the urge to go and share it with her. So after brushing his teeth, he went to knock on Flower's bedroom door to share the dream with her.

Flower answer by saying, "Come in John, I'm awake."

John opened the door and looked at Flower, who was still dressed in her new pink pajamas. He sat down beside her on the bed. He looked at her and said, "I had a very unusual dream last night and you were in it. In the dream you were crying to God about not understanding why so many people were starving."

"That's amazing because last night, to be honest, my heart was so troubled after seeing so many children starving. I'd never seen that before. Tell me more about the dream."

"Okay, I will do my best to communicate what God told me to tell you in the dream. This is what He said to me, 'If everyone was rich in the world, how could anyone understand what love is and how important it is to have it in our lives in order to be happy. I have given a mixture of blessings to all my people. Some people I blessed with a lot in this world, while others I blessed with less. The sad part is that those I blessed with a lot are often only willing to give a little. While the ones I blessed with little are often willing to give a lot. As you can see the balance is wrong. The only way for the balance to become right, is for everyone to work in unity to make the world a better place, by letting love guide your steps.'

"To be honest with you Flower, since I met you, you've helped me look differently at people and the purpose of living. So, my advice to you is to let go of the things you can't understand or explain. Just accept it if it can't be changed, or it will eat you up and destroy you. I was not willing to accept not being able to give my wife a child. The truth is that it was not in my hands to change or fix and therefore the situation left me without the understanding of why this must be.

"After coming here and meeting you I have a much stronger faith in God. Today, I truly believe, that what we see as bad, is in reality for something good in the end. I am not the wisest man, so tell me if I'm wrong. I hope these words have encouraged you, just as you have encouraged me."

"Yes, I can see that God's love has truly touched your heart. When we give to someone we know, it's easy to expect something back, both from the one who gives and from the one who receives. But when you give love to someone whom you do not know, especially if you have never seen that person before, you can expect nothing back. This gives a freedom to both because you know that you will most likely never see each other again, and therefore there is no need of wondering what you will receive or feel obligated to give to the other.

"So let's accept that there will be many poor people around us wherever we might go today. Let's not be sad for seeing them all, but rather be glad that we have been blessed to not live like that and therefore let us love them even more. For the purpose of life isn't to build on our understanding on things but to ask ourselves why because of it. Instead, life should be about giving at all times to everyone when you have an opportunity to make a difference in someone's life."

"Oh… Flower, I have been so blind for so long. Having so much and always wanting more made me very blind. I have found happiness in having nothing while being here. It has helped take away my blindness and now I can see clearly what matters the most. It's not what we have, but rather what we are willing to give to each other: love.

"I can't believe how late we slept this morning! It's already twelve-thirty and we are supposed to be at the reception at one o'clock to find out about our surprise. Let's hurry up and get ready, so we're not late. I love surprises."

They went down to meet the receptionist from yesterday. As they left the elevator and began to walk toward the reception, they noticed a lady with a big smile on her face. The first words to come out of her mouth as they reached the counter were, "Are you ready to enjoy your surprise?"

"Yes," John answered, "If you can fill in the blanks and let us know what kind of surprise it is."

"It's a very relaxing surprise. You may even fall asleep and wake up to feel like a new person."

Losing his patience, he said, "Come on lady, tell us the surprise or I'll leave right now."

"It's a massage, but not just any massage. It's a hot-stone massage. Your whole body will be lathered with hot oil and hot stones will be placed on the parts that will be massaged."

"That sounds very nice, but I have an injury in my chest. I suppose the person giving me the massage can work around it," he responded.

"Follow me and I will take you both to the massage room." The woman opened the door of the massage room, located next to the elevator. They walked inside and were greeted by the two women who were going to massage them.

With a nervous look on Flower's face she asked him, "John, does a massage hurt?"

"I will let you find out on your own, that way, there's still a surprise. But I can tell you this, you will not die."

Smiling, Flower said, "Thanks a lot for all your help." They stood in a big square room that was decorated like a wild jungle. The room was covered with real trees that had been planted in big flowerpots. Every tree had orchids with beautiful flowers, which had been grafted in with the tree as one. They even had vines hanging from the trees. There were also smaller plants and flowers that had been mixed in between the bigger trees.

Whoever had made this room had done a very good job. It really looked like a jungle. In the background you could hear soft music playing with the sounds of birds singing beautifully. It was very soothing for the soul.

One of the masseuses came and got Flower and took her to the opposite side of the jungle room, behind some of the jungle trees. They were told to get undressed down to their underwear and to lie on their stomachs on the massage bed. Flower and John could no longer see each other, even if they tried, because of the trees blocking their view. Their journey of relaxation for an hour began when the masseuse began to massage John. The soft hands and hot oil felt so good on his sore body.

With his eyes closed, John began to think of his wife massaging him and it put him to sleep.

Flower's nervousness over what to expect left as soon as the woman started to massage her. Flower loved the feeling of getting massaged. As the lady massaged her, Flower felt heavier and heavier and became so relaxed that she fell asleep just like John did.

Before they knew it, the massage was over. The next thing they needed to do was to go see the doctor. The doctor had forgotten to leave them the address for the clinic, so John asked the woman in reception if he could use the phone to call the doctor.

"You sure can. By the way, the massage must have treated you well. You both have better smiles on your faces than when you went in."

"Yes ma'am, I feel great. And I would like to apologize for running out of patience with you earlier."

"That's okay sir, I can be a real tease sometimes. Here is a phone for you to make your call."

"Thank you, ma'am." John called Doctor Kumar and a woman answered the phone. John told her that he needed the address for the clinic and she replied, "Oh, you are the man from yesterday. The doctor told me if you call to get him on the phone, so excuse me for a moment while I go and get the doctor for you."

"Hello, Mr. John, what can I do for you?"

"Well Doctor Kumar, yesterday you forgot to give me the address to your clinic."

"I'm so sorry John. I had so much on my mind yesterday. I guess it was a good thing that I left my phone number with you. Do you have a pen and a paper to write down the address?"

"Yes doctor, go for it."

After giving John the address, the doctor told him that the easiest and fastest way to his clinic would be to take a taxi. After finishing their conversation, Flower and John walked outside the hotel and took a taxi. It was a short ride with many turns. Their ride reached their destination and they walked into the doctor's office. A nurse greeted them and took them to the doctor. The first thing the doctor asked John was, "Did you like the surprise?"

"First of all, I want to thank you, doctor. I knew that it was you who set it up, as well as the dinner last night at the restaurant. I think I can speak for us both, knowing that it was Flower's first massage, that it was the best massage we'd ever experienced. And thank you for the clothes you provided for us, to look our best, at such a nice restaurant. I wish you could have seen Flower in that beautiful dress; she looked like an angel. It was a very special evening for both of us, so once again, thank you so much for everything."

"I will give your wound a look and then you can both be on your way to enjoy this day together. Since you both are Christians, I believe you would enjoy seeing a church that is located not far from here."

John looked at Flower and asked her, "Have you ever been inside a church?"

"I have seen a church from a distance, but I have never been inside one. I would love to see how a church looks from the inside. Do you mind if we go and see the church first?"

"Not at all, Flower. I would like to go to the church to pray and to give thanks to God for bringing you into my life."

The doctor said to John, "Here is some more money. You can take a taxi to the church and wherever you decide to go afterward."

They left the doctor's office and jumped into a taxi

and were on their way to the church. While driving along in the taxi, Flower took John's hand and held it for the first time. They both felt so happy being together. They looked around at the scenery, with their hearts full of joy and peace, enjoying each other's company. Before they knew it, they were at the church. They left the taxi and began to walk toward the entrance door. John grabbed the handle of the door that was about three meters high, pulled it open, and walked inside to explore the beautiful old church.

The windows of the church were tall and had a rectangular shape and their tops were oval, about one meter wide. The windows were dressed with stained glass in many different colors. When the sun shone on the glass, different shades of light appeared inside the church and made it feel like a holy place. The ceiling of the church was so high above the floor that it made their voices echo throughout the stone building when they spoke.

There were benches placed on each side of the walkway leading up to the altar, located in the center, opposite the church's entrance. The altar was made out of wood, and a big wooden cross hung about three meters above the floor. The cross represented the way Christ died for the world, and in return how we must die to ourselves, through faith in Christ, in order to receive the righteousness of God.

A stand was placed in the front beside the altar in order to kneel down and pray if you liked. They walked up to the stand, kneeled down on it and Flower said to John, "Let's pray and give thanks to the Lord."

She prayed, "Father God, I come before You today to

give You thanks for taking away the fear of not knowing if I would ever have someone to love me again. When my parents were taken away from me, the fear of loneliness entered my heart, which I had never tasted before. My father made me feel so loved and protected. The day he left my life, I was very angry with You God. Forgive me Father God, for You provide all my needs. All this time in the jungle, You have given me peace and joy like I have never felt before. I have been praying every day for You to bring someone into my life who I can love and have as a friend. I know in my heart that You have blessed me in a big way, when You brought John into my lonely life. I want to thank You, for him loving me the way he does. I also want to thank You for my first experience, to kneel down and pray to You on holy ground. I ask You to bless my relationship together with John and that You will provide a way for us to live together as a family. In Jesus name I pray, Amen."

After wiping away his tears, John prayed, "Father God, I don't know where to start, but let me begin by saying thank You, for all You have done in the past, for what You are doing in my life right now and for what You will do in my life. Thank You for healing me from blindness and allowing me to see life through Your eyes, because Your love is better than life. Thank You Father God, for You have revealed to me the purpose of life. For those who know Your name will trust in You, for You Lord have never forsaken those who seek You. Thank You for providing a way for me to know Your name, by coming to this part of the world and to find myself in You. Thank You for the blessed peace You brought in to my life, by

Flower coming into my life. I just want to say thank You, for all Your love that You are giving me, in Jesus' name I pray, Amen."

After they finished praying, they both had to wipe the tears of joy from their faces. It was moving and powerful to humble themselves and pray together with sincere hearts, full of thankfulness, knowing what God had done for them.

After their prayer together, John opened the door to the church and they stepped outside. He asked Flower, "Would you like to go for a walk?"

"Yes, I would love to," said Flower, with a big smile. The church they'd just visited was located on the outskirts of the city. They left the church and began to walk on a dirt road that led to the inner city. After they'd been walking for a while, they noticed a big crowd of people surrounding a section of the road ahead of them.

Being curious, both of them ran up to where all of the people were gathered to see what the commotion was all about. They worked their way through the crowd to see what had happened. To their surprise, it was a little girl around Flower's age. It appeared that she'd been driving a wagon pulled by a mule, when the wagon wheel came off. The wheel that broke off was on the same side of the road as a ditch. The girl fell off the wagon and into the ditch. The axle, without the wheel on it, had fallen on the girl's chest and she was in a lot of pain. A piece of metal from the wagon was buried in the girl's chest.

Many women were screaming in chaos at seeing the girl. Everyone was scared to move the wagon, fearing that the piece of metal would rip her apart. John advised

Flower to speak to the people in their language, to give them directions to help him lift the wagon off of the girl.

"Tell the men to lift at the same time on the count of three."

One, two, three and up went the wagon. The girl screamed in pain as the wagon, along with the metal piece, was pulled out of her chest. John quickly ran over and put pressure on the puncture wound with his hand and tried to stop the bleeding. They were all overwhelmed with compassion, tears on their faces, as the girl said over and over again, "I don't want to die."

These words reminded Flower of her father and how many times she had seen him ask people to receive salvation through God's Son, Jesus Christ. Flower looked at the girl in her eyes, eyes full of fear, and asked her name.

The girl responded to Flower, "My name is Anila."

"That is a beautiful name; do you know what it means?"

"It means 'child of the wind.'"

"My father always told me, 'It is never too late to receive God into your heart, as long as you do it before you die.' He also said that God is waiting for His children to come back home to Him, but they can only come back home if they willingly want to, because God will not force anyone to do something against their own will."

Anila grabbed Flower's arm and said to her, "I don't want to die."

What Flower didn't realize was that God's grace had been poured into her and that He was using her as an instrument to save Anila's soul.

Flower asked Anila, "Do you believe that there is good and evil in this world?"

Anila answered "I know that there is evil and good in this world."

The next question from Flower was, "Do you believe that you are going to a good place when you die?"

"Yes, I believe that I will."

"Why then are you so scared of dying, if you believe that you are going to a good place?"

"I believe, but I don't know."

Flower said, "You are fearful of dying because you don't know for sure where you are going. Do you want to be sure of where you are going when you die? There is a way to know where you will go."

"Yes please, show me the way. Knowing where I'm going will take away my fear of dying."

Flower continued with these words, "The only way to come to a better place, which is called the Kingdom of God, is to believe in God who created the heaven and the earth and all that is in them. You only have to believe that God gave His only begotten Son to die for our sins and whoever believes in Him, shall not perish, but have everlasting life. I can help you, if you close your eyes and pray these words with me."

Flower began to pray and Anila repeated these words, "Father God, forgive me for all my sins. I accept Jesus Christ as my Lord and Savior, to come into my life, and I believe in my heart, that God raised Him from the dead. In Jesus' name I pray, Amen."

When Flower finished praying and opened her eyes, Anila was not the same person. Anila's face was no longer full of fear, but was now glowing with peace from receiving God's love into her heart, by the Holy Spirit.

Anila said to Flower, "I am not afraid of dying anymore. I can't explain it, but I know in my heart that I am going to be with God."

Those were Anila's last words, with a big smile on her face, as she left them and went to be with the Lord. Flower looked at John and said "I feel so blessed because I understand why my father came home and was extra happy when he said to my mother, 'Today has been a glorious day, for God used me to help someone receive Christ. I know that the angels of heaven are rejoicing for a sinner who has turned from the error of his way has begun to live by bringing glory to God.'"

Flower and John both felt so blessed to see God at work. John felt led in his heart to pay for Anila's funeral. He asked around in the crowd for a cell phone and finally someone came forward to let him use one. He called Doctor Kumar and explained what had happened to Anila. He wanted to set up a funeral for the girl and pay the doctor back as soon as he was able to get his passport.

Doctor Kumar replied, "That is very nice of you, John. I understand that it would mean a lot for you to provide a funeral for Anila. I will call an ambulance to pick up her body and arrange a funeral for the girl. I would greatly appreciate it if you and Flower could wait there until the ambulance arrives."

"Of course, we will wait for the ambulance, and thank you so much for having such an understanding heart. I am sorry to interrupt your work, but I felt this was very important."

"Most certainly John, I am glad that you called and that I could help you. I understand why Flower is so fond of you, for you have a very kind and loving heart, which is a pretty rare quality among people today."

"Once again Doctor Kumar, thank you for everything and we will see you tomorrow at noon at the hotel."

While they waited for the ambulance, the girl's parents showed up. They sat down beside their daughter and cried in agony over how they'd just lost their only child to a foolish accident like this.

Watching these parents lose their child made Flower think about how she'd lost her parents. She knew the road of emotional recovery would be long and painful for these parents. After giving them a few minutes to collect themselves, Flower walked up to them and comforted them the best way she could, saying, "She died with peace in her heart and a smile on her face. She left to go and be with God."

These words touched the mother of Anila. She replied to Flower, "Thank you so much. It means a lot to me to know that my daughter died in peace."

John cut in and told Flower, "Tell the mother that I will pay for the funeral."

Flower translated to the mother what he wanted to do for her. She stood and walked to him and began to hug him hard, without letting go. She wept very hard and at the same time told John over and over again, according to Flower, "Thank you, thank you, thank you, for letting my daughter die with honor by giving her a complete funeral. My husband and I would never be able to pay for a funeral."

The ambulance arrived to pick up Anila's body. They left Anila's parents and went separate ways. Their hearts were full of sadness, knowing that Anila's parents had lost their only child at such young age.

At the same time, their hearts were full of joy and peace, knowing where Anila had gone. John looked at his watch and said, "Well, it's been a very rich day full of surprises and time has gone by quickly. It's already six o'clock and I'm starving. Why don't we go back to the hotel and eat dinner?"

"That sounds like a great idea. I'm starving too," Flower replied.

"Let's take the taxi that is parked over there." They gave the name of their hotel to the driver and were on their way to their hotel.

Once they arrived, they went to their room to take a shower and get cleaned up before getting dressed for dinner.

While sitting at the dinner table John asked Flower, "Would you like to go for a swim after dinner?"

"I would love to," Flower answered. "Believe it or not, the only swimming pool I have ever used was the river. I'm really looking forward to swimming in a real pool for the first time."

After dinner, they went back upstairs to their room to change and dress in their bathing suits, which they'd rented at the reception desk. With a robe around them, they took the elevator to go back down to the first floor and outside to enjoy the pool together. John enjoyed the moment, watching Flower float around in the pool on an inflated mattress, with a smile full of happiness.

John thought back on what had happened earlier in the day. How when a girl faced death with fear, God used Flower to turn the situation around. At that moment, Flower came out of the pool and sat down next to him. She asked, "Would you like to swim with me?"

"I'm just reflecting on what happened earlier today. I understand that God used you to help the girl. I really envy you. You are always so full of life and radiating love with a constant smile on your face. I wish I could love the way you love life and people. The most amazing thing to me about all this is the way you lost your parents but still haven't given up on love. I hope that one day I can learn how to love the way you love."

"You can, John. We can all learn to love in a way that is pleasing to God. The biggest secret to having a loving heart is to put perfect love into it. Our love is not perfect but God's love is. To love perfectly is to allow God to teach you how to love, like He loves. The first three months in the jungle, I lived in despair. I was so broken and felt so weak. I lost all my dreams that had given me hope and a desire to live. When I felt lost and my spirit felt totally crushed, God never left my side. I learned to trust in God. I decided that I really wanted to know God and His love more deeply. I went back to the guesthouse to get a Bible. I was determined to seek God with all my heart. The more I searched God through His Word, the more truth He revealed to me regarding the gift of life and how His love is better than life and how strongly He loves us all."

By memory Florence quoted these verses from the Bible to John: "Jeremiah 29:11-13 says, 'For I know the plans I have for you declares the Lord, plans to prosper you and not to harm you, plans to give you hope and a future. Then you will call upon me and come and pray to me, and I will listen to you. You will seek me and you will find me when you seek me with all your heart.'"

Amazed, John said, "Wow, you really know these verses by heart."

"Every time I needed courage, I read these verses and by doing so, I believed that God had a plan for me, even when I was on my own. While my faith grew stronger, so did my hope for a better future. 'For faith is being sure of what we hope for and certain of what we do not see.' My hope grew stronger that someday someone would come into my life who I could love and have as a friend. Then one day, you came into my life. John. I believe that you were a plan of God and not a mistake. You were the missing link to me feeling alive and having purpose for living again. I really have a desire in my heart to be your adopted daughter and to meet your wife and family."

"Regardless of what I have been through by coming here Flower, I have never felt so strongly in my heart that our connection is meant to be. I have always believed that your life can change, for the better or worse, depending on who you meet in life. This may sound crazy but I can't deny what my heart feels about you. My whole family will love you and I know that you will be an inspiration to them as well."

Flower asked, "How many brothers and sisters do you have?"

"I have one sister named Sofia. Her husband's name is David. Sofia is thirty-eight years-old and her husband is forty years-old. They have one son by the name of Samuel and he is eight years-old. I have two brothers and they are both older than I am. My oldest brother, Sam, is forty years-old and his wife Victoria is thirty-four years-old. They have a daughter also named Victoria. My brother wanted his first child to be named after his wife. Their daughter Victoria is the same age as you and you will really like her. She has a special talent, which I believe is a gift from God. Victoria is an artist who paints pictures and does it very well. My middle brother's name is Joe and his wife's name is Mary. Joe is thirty-seven years-old and Mary is thirty-six years-old. They have a son by the name of Charles and he is seven years-old. I could tell you the personalities of my whole family, but I want my wife to tell you all about them. That way you have something to look forward to with my wife.

"Oh, and we can't leave my parents out. My father's name is Philip and he is seventy years-old. My mother's name is Susan and she is sixty-seven years-old. Florence, you have opened a new door in my life. Once again it's filled with the same dream that I once used to have, the dream of having my own family. To me there is no family unless there is a child in it. I think you will love England. You will not see people begging for food, like here. You will feel like you are entering a new world, with all kinds of technology surrounding you wherever you go.

"Your parents made a choice to live a simple life, by coming here and living in the countryside of India. Coming here and being on my own for the first time has helped me to understand the most important thing in life, to have someone who cares for you. For the things of the world do not encourage you when you feel down and broken, but a true friend can do that for you. How you live is how you feel.

"Alright, I've have enjoyed our conversation and what we both experienced together earlier today, but I think it's time for us to go to bed. Are you ready for bed, or do you want to enjoy the pool little longer?"

"Yes, let's go to bed. I am very tired after a busy day."

After a good night's sleep, Flower woke up first and jumped into the shower. Her singing in the shower woke John up. "What a beautiful voice she has," he thought to himself. Still lying in the bed, woken with a smile on his face, John said out loud to himself, "I wouldn't mind waking up like this every morning."

Encouraged by Flower, John began to sing too, while starting a new day with his own morning shower. They both finished their showers and got dressed at the same time. When they walked out of their bedrooms, their eyes met and they both smiled at each other. Flower said, "Someone woke up extra happy this morning."

"Look who's talking! I've never heard you sing before and you're really good at it. You have a beautiful singing voice. It was so nice waking up listening to your singing. It made me sing too, and I can't sing for nothing. For some reason, I really enjoyed it anyway. My stomach is growling for some breakfast. Do you feel the same?"

"Yes, let's go downstairs and have some breakfast."

So they walked out of the elevator onto the first floor and, as they passed the receptionist, she said to John, "Mister John, I have something to share with you, but only for you."

Flower stepped back to give them privacy. The woman who surprised them the day before had a new surprise to share with John, but this time it was addressed only to Flower. The receptionist told him that the doctor called earlier that morning and wanted to give Flower the gift of her first manicure.

John replied, "I like the surprise a lot. I'll bring her to the reception after we are done with breakfast."

"Yes Mister John, I will take care of her and bring her to the the spa."

"Thank you, ma'am. I don't know why, but I'm so excited on Flower's behalf. Thank you so much for telling me without letting her know."

With a big smile on his face, he turned around, looked at Flower and said, "You're really going to enjoy your breakfast."

"Why is that?"

"I will tell you at the breakfast table."

After they collected their breakfast plates from the buffet and sat down, Flower was quick to ask him, "Why am I going to enjoy my breakfast so much?"

"You have a surprise waiting for you at the reception after breakfast." John laughed as he watched Flower speed up her eating.

"Slow down, Flower, you're not going before I'm done eating. I have to bring you to reception."

"Well, hurry up. I remember how much you enjoyed your surprise last time, so have some compassion on me for being eager to get there."

"Okay, you can go, but remember to tell the lady that I said it was okay for you to go alone."

"Thank you so much! I love you, John! I will go straight up to my room after my surprise." Flower left John by himself and new thoughts entered his mind. His first thought was about how great the breakfast was. Not because of the food, but because of how he felt, in a way that he'd never felt before. The feeling of being loved as a parent, of hearing the words from a child telling you, "I love you."

He had been waiting for a sign from God to confirm that Flower and he belonged together as a family. When Flower said, "I love you, John," it really hit his heart, like a key was put into it. He bowed his head at the breakfast table and said to God, "Thank You, God, for showing me the sign I asked for earlier, for me and Flower to be together or not. Thank You for letting me know this early and therefore bringing peace to my heart."

He finished his breakfast and went up to his room and began to read his Bible.

Meanwhile, Flower was enjoying her first manicure.

The woman doing Flower's nails asked her, "What is your favorite color? Would you like this color on your nails?"

"My favorite color is light blue and I would love to see my nails done in that color." Flower admired her nails being transformed from dirty to beautiful.

When the woman was done with her nails, she asked Flower, "Would you like to have your hair done as well?"

"I would love to. It's been so long since I had my hair done." The hairdresser took Flower by the hand and led her to a special chair. The hairdresser washed Flower's hair. Then the hairdresser suggested that Flower cut her hair shorter because her bangs were badly damaged.

"It would be good for your hair and it will give you a nicer look. I could also cut your bangs shorter so that your beautiful smile can be revealed." Flower was nervous that she might not like her new look, but gave the okay for the woman to cut her hair.

Flower broke in her new look with a smile of approval. Trimming away so much hair made her head feel much lighter. She hoped that John would like it as well. "Thank you for a great job," Flower said. She rushed back up to her room to see if John would approve her new look.

Flower grabbed the doorknob and paused to make sure that her hair looked its best. She hoped to get a warm greeting from John.

Flower opened the door and walked in. John stood up from his seat on the couch and walked toward Flower to greet this new girl. He put his hands on her shoulders and looked into her eyes and said, "What a blessed man I am to have such a beautiful girl, both in looks and heart. I love your new look and now I can see your smile all the time. You can no longer hide your beautiful face behind that long hair. You must be happy with how your hair turned out."

"Thank you. I was so nervous that you wouldn't like it."

"Well Flower, my approval for you is always secure and the same. By the way, Doctor Kumar should be here any moment to drive us back home. The time is eleven-thirty and we must be no later than noon. Believe me when I say that Doctor Kumar, Uma, and the whole town will approve of your new look. Let's pack our stuff and go downstairs and wait for him at the reception."

They packed the few things they had and went down to the reception area. They sat down on a sofa and waited for Doctor Kumar to come. Five minutes later he walked in with a smile on his face and said, "What a lovely pair sitting here."

"I told you that he would love your new look," John said to Flower.

After Doctor Kumar paid the tab for their stay at the hotel they left and walked to his car and their journey back home started. In the car, Flower said, "I want to thank you from the bottom of my heart, for allowing me to experience so many new things. Today I feel like the girl I once used to be. You gave us a wonderful time together. I truly enjoyed our dinner with the beautiful dress you provided for me to wear. I felt like a princess going to dinner with a handsome prince. That massage took me to another world of pleasure and to finish it all, you gave me a new look that I like a lot. Thank you for everything, Doctor Kumar, for these memories will always be with me."

John added, "During our time in the city, Flower taught me that life is not given to you to live for yourself, but to live for others. When you live for yourself, you easily become selfish and compare yourself with others. When you learn to live for others, you begin to see their needs and not their flaws. Never in my life would I have dreamed that a twelve year-old girl would affect my life in such rich way.

"I'm glad that God brought Flower into my life and

corrected my way of living and thinking toward people. The connection between us is so strong that it feels like we have known each other for a long time. So thank you, Doctor Kumar, for providing a way for me and Flower to get to know each other in a deeper way."

Then Doctor Kumar said, "You and Flower are both welcome. You are special people to me and you belong with each other. By the way, John, how do you feel regarding your health?"

"I feel great," John answered.

Flower asked Doctor Kumar, "How much longer before we are home?"

"We should be back home in about half an hour." The rich conversations they shared made the time pass quickly. They all enjoyed the ride in his old classic car, with its convertible top down and the wind blowing on them.

When they arrived in their town, everyone came running toward them to take a look at Doctor Kumar's antique car. When Uma came with Toby, Flower ran up to Toby with tears in her eyes. She hugged his big head and said, "I have missed you so much that my heart has been hurting the whole time we've been apart. I hope I never have to be away from you again, Toby."

Then Uma said to Flower, "I have missed you so much! And I really like your new look."

Flower hugged Uma and said, "Thank you. I'm very happy that you like my new look. I wish you could've been with us. We experienced such great things together."

Doctor Kumar turned to Uma and said, "I am sorry but I cannot stay. I have to leave right away to see a client not too far away from here, then I must go back home. John has my phone number in case of an emergency."

They all said goodbye to the doctor and sent him on his way. "Until I see you next time, take care of my special girl," he said, and then he was gone. Flower and John couldn't wait to tell Uma their great stories from the trip.

"Well, you must both be starving after a long drive. Let's go up to the guesthouse and make dinner. I'm curious to hear your stories and to hear how the big city treated you both."

Flower and John rode Toby back to the guesthouse and Uma walked next to Toby. As Toby reached the guesthouse, to Flower's amazement, she could see that the house was nearly finished, and certainly livable.

Flower said to Uma, "These last days have been like a dream and I felt like a princess. Now to see my new house truly makes me feel like a dream has come true."

After they finished inspecting the new house, Flower took Toby for a ride in the jungle, while Uma and John went to the guesthouse to cook dinner and talk about what they had experienced together the last few days in the big city.

Uma said to John in the kitchen, "I was hoping to have the house completely done before you returned back home again."

"That can be arranged, Uma, if you agree with what I'm about to suggest. We can all three go together with Toby and ride to the temple I told you about, where Flower and Toby were living for almost a year. You must see what they've done with the place. I can't describe the beauty of it in words; it can only be experienced by being there in person. Believe me, you will not regret going after you see the beautiful flower arrangements Flower has done in that place. No harm will come our way because Toby will protect us from any wild animals in the jungle. So what do you say Uma? You only live once, as I have been taught by Flower."

"Since you put it in so many nice words, I can't say no to you. Let's do it."

While cooking dinner together, John shared some special moments that he had experienced with Flower in the big city.

"The best moment for me, aside from the way Flower encouraged the dying girl I shared about earlier, was when Flower looked at me and said, 'I love you, John.' For the first time in my life, I tasted what it feels to be a parent."

"Anyone can see that you both belong together. God brought you together."

John asked Uma, "How was Flower's father as a person?"

Uma answered, "He was a soft-spoken man filled with words of wisdom from God. He knew the scriptures from the Bible by heart and every time he spoke with you about God, he left you with a desire to want to learn more about Him. Simon told me to be prepared, for there are many people and religions, and all believe that their faith is true. He also told me, 'We live and act upon the faith we have, so our actions toward people will speak louder than words.' You will live in the way you feel in your heart. If you always complain about how bad life is and how bad people are, you should ask yourself if your faith is the right faith. After all, faith comes from what you believe.' Simon told me to try to learn to store the Word of God in my heart by remembering verses. 'The only thing that counts is faith expressing itself through love.' When we have the faith of Christ in our hearts, only then can we learn to love all people the same without passing judgment."

"I can tell that Simon was a very wise man," John said. "All I have to do is look at Flower and see what a good job he did teaching her how to treat people, by expressing herself with God's perfect love in her heart."

Just then, Flower walked in, sat down by the kitchen table, and joined the conversation. John was quick to share the good news with Flower, "Uma has agreed to go with us to the temple and also to spend a night over there. That way, your new house should be done by the time we come back. I hope you don't disagree, Flower."

"I would never turn down an offer like that. I know how much Uma will like this place."

"Okay," John said, "that is great. Now we can enjoy dinner and have something to look forward to. I can't wait to see the reaction on Uma's face when she sees how beautiful the temple really is."

After dinner, Flower and John spent a couple of hours sharing more stories with Uma from their time in the big city. By eleven o'clock they were all asleep.

An Elephant Ride
and a Big Surprise

Uma woke up first with the sunrise. Excited and restless to leave on the trip to the temple, Uma prepared breakfast for everyone. After breakfast, Uma went to get Kalyani, her niece, in order to tell her to take care of the guesthouse until Uma returned.

They packed some things and loaded them onto Toby. Together they rode into the wild jungle. After riding Toby for some time, they took a break and sat down on the ground to eat their lunch. They finished eating the sandwiches Uma had made for them and then continued their journey to the temple.

A little while later they heard a roar. This was not a sound that anyone wanted to hear. It was the roar of a hungry tiger looking for something to eat. Flower told Toby to stop walking and to wait for the roar of the tiger to end. All three of them sat on Toby's back fearful that the tiger would come near them.

In that very moment, when their hearts felt like exploding, the tiger jumped out right in front of them. They all shouted at the same time. Toby blew his trunk louder than ever before and began to charge the tiger.

Most likely because of Toby's aggressive approach, the tiger turned around and ran back into the jungle. Uma was the first to speak after the tiger left and said, "That was without a doubt the scariest moment of my entire life. What do you say Flower?"

"I have encountered a tiger twice before today, and yes, the first time felt like I swallowed my own heart in fear. I was scared, but since Toby protected me before, I trusted him to do the same today and I was right. Now you both know how I survived in the jungle by myself."

Uma said, "No wonder why you love Toby so much. He has rescued you from death three times and this experience has only made me love Toby more as well."

The ride continued, and as their hearts slowly returned to normal, they were all happy to still be alive. After a few hours of riding, they finally saw the entrance of the temple. They entered the temple and were met with a surprise. It was full of monkeys.

The monkeys had made a big mess inside the temple. Flower's personal things were everywhere. Flower quickly got down to the ground and screamed at the monkeys, scaring them off. With tears streaming down her face, Flower walked up and hugged John, saying with pain in her heart, "Look John! The monkeys have destroyed everything! Toby and I have worked so hard to make this place into a beautiful home. They have even pulled out all the orchids from my beautiful tree. I don't understand, John. Why did this happen now and not before?"

Uma cut in and said to Flower, "Let me remind you of what your father used to say regarding things we don't understand as Christians. He always talked about God opening and closing doors through our lives. When we give ourselves completely to Christ, we begin our journey of faith in Christ. He molds us and shapes us into His likeness, by allowing us to experience situations we do not like. Your faith doesn't grow stronger when things go well, but rather when you have to face things you do not like. When our faith becomes strong enough, we don't question His ways. God says in His Word, 'For my thoughts are not your thoughts, neither are your ways my ways.' Today I also love Him more than anything, because I know that I can trust Him."

"Isn't love built on trust, Uma?" asked Flower through her tears.

"Yes it is, Flower. Without trust, a relationship will not last and God doesn't want us to give up, for He will not give up on us. I have no doubt that God has big plans for you, Flower. You shared with me last night the story of the dying girl and God showed you that your purpose for living is to save lost souls. How can we be saved, if all we want to do is to live for ourselves? When we receive the love of Christ in our hearts, we begin to learn to love everyone. We want to help people find the love of God in their hearts by sharing the Word of God and what He has done for us. We do this by sharing our own testimony, about what God has done for us. I don't believe that God wants part of your heart to long for this place, but that your whole heart will be ready to go wherever God might send you, in order to do His will.

"I'm not saying that it's wrong to miss a place, as long as it doesn't bring an effort to please your own desires first. Always live to do God's will first. For this world and its desires will pass away, but the man who does the will of God lives forever. I hope these words have helped and encouraged you to understand that all things happen for a reason.

"Flower, I can see that this place is beautiful and I know that you were longing for me to see it looking its best. Don't be upset. Instead, let's be thankful that God was protecting you in such a beautiful place with a personal bodyguard in Toby."

"Oh Uma, you've always had a way of picking me up when I feel down."

"Well, I've been blessed with two teachers who taught me how to encourage people. Simon in person and God in Spirit. Let's work together and see if we can turn this place back to the way it used to look, before the monkeys had their fun and made it a mess." They all worked hard together and made Flower's temple presentable again.

Meanwhile, back home in the town, the people received a big surprise. After being gone for three years in the navy, having been around the world, Jack was home. He looked handsome in his uniform, complete with the navy hat on his head. He entered town and everyone greeted him and welcomed him back home.

Jack looked for Uma and his sister, Florence. When he couldn't find them he asked a man nearby, "Where are Uma and Florence?"

The man pointed Jack to an apartment. "Knock on the door, the person inside can give you the information you need."

Jack walked up to the door and knocked. Uma's niece,

Kalyani, opened the door. Jack was speechless and stared at her for a moment. "Wow, you have really grown up and become a beautiful women," he said. "If I remember correctly, you were fifteen years-old when I left, which makes you eighteen years-old today, yes? You have changed so much during this time. That calls for a hug. Come here, Kalyani, and give me a hug."

When he hugged her, he felt touched in his heart and became attracted to her in a way he had never felt before. After they were done hugging, he couldn't stop looking at her. He hoped she didn't notice how much he was staring at her and feel uncomfortable.

His eyes just wanted to keep admiring her beauty and sweetness. She had grown tall and her body was fully shaped. Her hazel eyes matched her hair, which was straight and shone beautifully, hanging down past her bosom.

Jack and Kalyani were always close growing up and he had often wished that they could date each other. But because of their age difference, Jack refrained from asking her to be his girl. But now being an adult changed everything. And perhaps because of this he fell in love with her, for he had never felt like this before. When she looked at him and smiled, his heart tingled. He couldn't help hoping that she felt the same way about him.

With her soft and tender voice, Kalyani said, "I am so sorry for what happened to your parents. I know how close you were with them."

"Yeah… I miss them so much. I missed them so much more after receiving the letter from Uma, knowing that I'll never be able to see them again. Being away and having to stand on my own feet and enter the grown-up world has made me realize how blessed I've been all this time to have such wonderful parents. They were a good influence on my life. Because of them, I am the man I am today. They both had their own way of describing the love of God and how important love is for us all. I will never forget the words my mom shared with me on the day I left for the navy. She told me, 'Be careful, Jack, when you go out in the world with its temptations. It is so easy to get lost by allowing other people to make your choices. Always be strong and firm and listen to yourself. It's better to walk away, then to take a chance and end up in trouble for making the wrong choice.'"

Then Jack said, "We are so quick to forget what we have. Instead we see what we could have. Therefore it's hard to be content. All I cared about three years ago was joining the navy and exploring the world. I expected to see great things. All the while, the greatest thing in my life was at home all along, my loving parents. What about you, Kalyani, do you have someone special in your life?"

"My special person is Uma. My parents wanted me to marry an old man. That was pleasing them, but not to me. I asked Uma to help my mother understand how unhappy I would be, to be forced to marry someone I didn't choose. That's the reason why I'm living with Uma. I hope one day that my parents will understand and agree that I can't marry someone I don't love. By the way Jack, you must wonder where your sister is."

"Yes, do you know where she is?"

"Florence, Uma, and John are in the jungle and will be back tomorrow."

Jack asked, "What are they doing in the jungle?"

"I don't know. All that Uma said was to take care of the guesthouse and that they would be back tomorrow. They left early this morning riding Florence's elephant."

"Elephant! When did my sister get an elephant?"

"You will find out tomorrow. I want Florence to tell you in person. By the way, Florence's new name is Flower. John gave it to her as a nickname. You must be hungry, Jack. Let's walk up to the guesthouse so I can cook dinner for us. There is a surprise for you to see next to the guesthouse and I think you will like it."

They walked up to the guesthouse together.

Kalyani looked at Jack and thought to herself, "When Jack left he was a skinny guy, but today he looks like a man, with a nice muscular body." Jack's height reached about 180 centimeters. His blond hair and beautiful blue eyes made her melt inside every time their eyes met. She noticed his thick eyebrows with long eyelashes and the oval shape of his face.

Jack looked at Kalyani who was about twenty centimeters shorter than he was. She wore a beautiful blue dress. The wind blowing around them as they walked outside brought her nice aroma to his attention. He'd never smelled something so sweet before. As they came up the hill toward the guesthouse, Jack could see something new being built behind it.

Being curious, he ran up ahead and stood next to the guesthouse, where he could see a new house being built where the old house once stood.

Jack asked Kalyani, "Who has built the house?"

She replied, "The people of the town wanted to give back the love that your parents always gave to them."

With tears in his eyes, Jack walked inside for a peek of the newly built house that honored his parents. He realized what a great impact they had made on this little town and its people. After they finished exploring the new house together, Jack and Kalyani entered the guesthouse. They went into the kitchen and started to cook dinner together, enjoying each other's company.

Back at the temple, being tired from the hard work of putting Florence's home in order again, John made a fire for everyone. They sat around it and relaxed for a moment before cooking dinner. Uma lay down on her back on top of a thick bed of leaves. She stretched her body, making herself as long as possible. It felt good to stretch after bending down for hours cleaning up the temple.

Uma looked around to admire the place. She said, "Isn't it beautiful to see how God provides for all our needs? God provided for you and Toby to live here. Instead of leaving this place, you looked at it and embraced its potential to be a home. You found a place where you could feel safer than sleeping out in the wild jungle. You embraced what God gave you and made it into a blessing. Many times, we are blind to see the blessing God has given us, because of the time that's required to make it happen. So God gave you a walking muscle filled with strength in the shape of an elephant. Many times we give up too early, while the blessing is waiting around the corner.

"John, if you wondered about the girl I put in charge of watching over the guesthouse, she is my niece, Kalyani. My sister wanted to force her to marry a rich man without her consent. I have taken her under my wings until her parents come to an agreement and put their daughter's feelings first, by letting her marry who she desire to marry."

"I'm so sorry to hear that, Uma," John replied. "My wish for her is that all she hopes for will come true."

"As long as she is in my care, it will be possible."

"You are a very kind and wise woman. I'm very happy that our road of life has crossed each other's and that we have come to know each other. It's not hard to understand why Flower is so close to you. You truly are a good friend to have."

"Thank you John, those words helps me to believe in myself and that what I am doing is right."

Flower cut into the conversation and said, "I'm sorry to interrupt, but we only have little daylight left, and I think we should prepare dinner while we still have it."

"You're right; we better get going if we are going to have our dinner done before it gets dark," said Uma.

Back in town, Jack and Kalyani finished cooking dinner. They began to eat their homemade chicken curry with rice and vegetables.

Jack said to Kalyani, "I have been waiting for three years to enjoy homemade food again. I love the way you have cooked the chicken, Kalyani."

"I give all the credit to Uma. She helped me become a better cook."

"I must thank Uma in person for doing such good job teaching you how to cook. Without any doubt, this is the best curry chicken I have ever tasted."

After dinner, Jack walked Kalyani back to her apartment. Standing by the door of Uma's apartment, before letting Kalyani go inside, Jack grabbed her shoulders, looked into her eyes, and said, "Thank you for a wonderful afternoon and a lovely dinner. This has been a nice reunion between us. If you want to, I would love to spend more time with you tomorrow."

"I would love to, Jack. What do you say if I come tomorrow morning at nine o'clock?"

"Sounds great," said Jack as he kissed her on her cheek and left.

Jack walked back to the guesthouse. He couldn't wait until tomorrow to spend more time with Kalyani. He hoped that she would tell him if she felt the same toward him.

A little later Joshi, the spokesman of the town, came and knocked on Kalyani's door. "We plan on having a big barbecue party tomorrow from noon until sunset, with all kinds of foods and juice all day long. Tomorrow at eleven in the morning, we will meet at the new house to prepare for the feast of celebrating Jack's return. Uma wanted it to be a surprise, so I was hoping that you could make a small lunch and take Jack for a picnic in the jungle, to keep him away so we can arrange everything for his surprise."

"Consider it done," Kalyani answered Joshi. "I can't wait to see Jack's expression when his surprise is revealed tomorrow."

Joshi left and Kalyani closed the door for the night. She went to sleep with excitement about what was about to happen tomorrow.

At the same time in the guesthouse, Jack grabbed a family photo album and began to think about his sister. Jack looked at a picture of when he and Florence were playing at the creek, not far from there, and began to long for his sister's presence. After going through the pictures, Jack fell asleep with a smile on his face.

The next morning at nine o'clock, Kalyani knocked on Jack's door to wake him. Jack had been up since six o'clock waiting for this knock on the door. He was so in love that it hurt. He couldn't get Kalyani's beautiful face out of his mind. All he could see last night when he closed his eyes was Kalyani's beautiful smile. Excited to get to know Kalyani more, Jack opened the door with a smile full of anticipation. Kalyani responded with a shy but confident smile.

"I'm glad that you're up," Kalyani said. "I hope that your first night's sleep back home was good. I know I slept good knowing that you are back home."

"Thank you," said Jack, thinking to himself, "She must really like me. If not, why would she say what she just said?" He hoped she could see in him more than just a friend. He knew that she was shy and that he must take it slowly or he might scare her away. They both went into the kitchen and sat down by the table.

"Kalyani, would you like to have some breakfast?" Jack asked.

"Tea would be fine, thank you. I've already had

breakfast." Jack made the tea and worked himself up to ask her a personal question.

"What are your plans for the future?"

"This town is a good place to live and the people are very nice. I like it here. Uma gave me a job picking the tea harvest and she is teaching me how to plant and prepare tea plants for planting. I know that it's not a rich man's job, what I do, but I really like it," she answered. "I don't need much to be content, but I look forward to falling in love with a man who will treat me good and who will love me for who I am. I also would love to have children one day.

"I had a dream to go to school and become a veterinarian because I love animals. They never complain and are always ready to love you, whether you have a good or bad day. It's nice to have dreams, even if they will never happen. The school is very expensive and I'm a poor girl. I will not give up my dream yet. I am young and you never know what the future holds for my life."

Jack thought to himself for a moment and reflected on what Kalyani just said about herself. She was a very determined person who would not give up on her desires. That showed a strength of knowing who she was and what she wanted. The way she spoke about animals showed that she had a big compassionate heart. In other words, she believed in love.

"What about you, Jack? Do you already have plans for your future?"

"To be honest with you, I don't know what I want right now. It felt like the whole world came crashing down on me when I received the letter from Uma regarding my parents' death. I feel bad that all I wanted to do was to leave and see the world, but now I wish I had stayed home. I could've spent two more years with them and could've shown them that I really love them. I feel guilty that I wasn't here to help them… to keep them from getting killed somehow."

"Oh, Jack, you shouldn't think that way. If you had been here, you might have been killed too. Then who would be there for Flower?"

"Thank you for the encouragement. I wish I had been more open to say the words, 'I love you,' while they were still alive. This incident with their death has made me realize the importance of showing love to the people you care for while they are still alive. They both told me all the time, 'I love you, Jack.' Instead of answering them in the same way, all I said was, 'Thank you.' I don't know why it was so hard for me to say those words. I felt the same way and I wanted to say 'I love you' to them as well. Maybe it was because they were not my birth parents, or maybe because it made me feel shy to hear those words being spoken to me. In the navy I realized the importance of having a family regardless of whether your parents were from birth or not. The importance of a family is in knowing that someone cares for you, like it would be for your own parents.

"Last night was the slowest night of my life. I couldn't sleep because I kept thinking about you and I couldn't wait for you to come. I couldn't wait for you to knock on my door this morning to see your beautiful smile again. What I'm trying to say is that I'm falling in love with you."

Kalyani blushed and took her time answering Jack. "Thank you for those words. They truly mean a lot to me and I'm so happy that you are back home." Kalyani looked at her watch and hoped that it was time to ask Jack to go for a walk, and therefore, to escape not knowing how to respond to Jack's words. She felt the urge to leave, even if it was too soon, due to the pressure of hearing his words.

Kalyani asked Jack "Would you like to go for a walk in the jungle with me?"

"I would love to. And we can go to the creek, where we used to go with my parents when we were young."

They left with a lunch basket and a blanket and walked toward the creek, which was located at the edge of the jungle, about half an hour away from the guesthouse.

Meanwhile, John, Flower, and Uma had already left the temple a few hours previous, and Uma's experience of riding an elephant was coming to an end.

Reaching the creek, Jack and Kalyani lay down on a blanket and looked up at the clouds. Kalyani thought to herself, "How am I going to tell Jack that I've always loved him but our age difference felt so big when we were younger? It kept me from coming to him in the way I wanted to."

But today it felt different. They were both grown-ups now.

After building up her courage, Kalyani said, "I am so nervous, but I must be honest with you. I have wanted to say this to you for as long as I remember us being friends. I love you, Jack, and I have always loved you since I first met you. I hope you are okay with this because I can't help feeling this way about you. Your beautiful blue eyes have made me melt inside for all these years, each time you looked at me during our years growing up. I love your smile and your laugh, because it makes me want to laugh. Don't we all have one common desire in life? To be happy?"

Jack reached over and pulled Kalyani toward him and kissed her. Then he said, "This is the best day of my life. To know that a beautiful woman like you has always loved me."

"Just like you, this is also the happiest day of my life."

While enjoying their first romance, their peace was interrupted by a loud sound coming toward them from the jungle. They grabbed the blanket and basket and took cover behind a fallen tree to wait and see who was coming.

To their surprise, it was Flower riding an elephant, along with John and Uma.

Jack allowed Toby to pass before he jumped out from the hiding place and shouted, "Surprise!"

Toby quickly turned around.

Flower shouted, "Jack! What are you doing here?"

Then Flower climbed down from Toby's back and walked to her brother. They greeted each other with hugs, and Flower cried tears of happiness for being back together with her brother.

Uma asked Jack, "Why are you home so early? In your letter you said that you would be back at Christmas, which is almost a week from now."

"When I received your letter, Uma, my heart was troubled over what happened to my parents. It also made me think about my sister and how she was holding together. So I talked to a higher ranked officer regarding my concern for Florence. I felt the need to come home and help her cope with our parents' death. The officer in charge had a good heart and he helped to make it happen, allowing me to come home one week sooner."

Then John walked up to Jack and said, "Hi, my name is John. Flower has told me great things about you and I'm glad to finally meet you. She's been through a lot, but thanks to her strong faith in God, she has made it through."

"That's my sister, John. Florence has always had a strong faith, as long as I can remember."

Uma gave Kalyani a hug and said to John, "This is my beautiful niece Kalyani.

We are both very happy for Flower to find a man figure like you to look up to." When Toby finished drinking from the creek, they all began to walk back home, as a big happy family.

At the same time, things had come together for Jack's welcome home party to begin. Several fires were lit for barbecue and food was cooking everywhere you looked. No one would leave this party with an empty stomach. People from the town were up on the hill by the guesthouse, singing together and full of joy knowing that Jack and Flower were together again.

Planning for
the Future

Back in the jungle, Jack and Flower walked side by side holding hands. They talked to each other and Jack could see that Flower was okay. This brought peace to his heart. He looked at his sister and said, "I am so blessed to have a great sister like you in my life."

"Thank you Jack. I am blessed as well to have a good brother like you." They talked to each other for a while. Not being too far from home, they could hear a commotion of music and singing. They finally reached the guesthouse and could see that there was party going on.

Joshi made everyone quiet down and said, "Look, Jack is home!"

Jack walked up to Joshi and asked him, "What is this all about?"

"It's to celebrate that you have come home safely. The whole family is complete now that you and Flower are smiling together again. Even if we know that Simon and Sheryl will never be here again."

Then Joshi said to Jack and Flower, "Now we are going to eat and celebrate Jack's homecoming and tonight you will enjoy sleeping in the new house, which is ready to be moved into."

Jack looked at John and said, "Wow, what a beautiful surprise! I never thought I would be able to feel so good coming home again. Today I understand the words my father once told me. He said that change takes time and many times we give up too early, because we don't have the patience to wait for change to happen. I feel so blessed seeing the change that has taken place among these people. My father always told me to never give up on love, for love will never give up on you.

"My parents left footprints of love. How I wish they could both be here to see the impact they made in this place. Their task is done. The roots of love have grown deep among these people. Now it is our duty to continue what my parents started."

After talking and sharing many stories, the party ended at sunset and all went home for the night. Uma suggested, "Why don't Jack and Flower go to their new home and spend some time together talking about the future. Me, John, and Kalyani are staying in the guesthouse, which has a room for each one of us. You can see Jack, that the new house is built only one story high and not two, like the old house. It has two bedrooms, one for you, Jack and one for Flower. It also has a kitchen, living room and a bathroom to share. We have placed a bed in each bedroom, along with a dresser for your clothes. Enjoy the night together and we will see each other again tomorrow morning."

Flower replied, "What about our things that are in the guesthouse?"

"You will both find your things in your bedroom. We left your belongings in boxes so that you can go through what you want to keep, and then you can organize your clothes and things the way you want."

Jack and Flower entered their new home and went into their bedrooms, after exploring the house, and began to organize their own bedrooms. In the guesthouse Kalyani asked Uma to speak with her in private. Uma said, "Yes," and they walked into Uma's bedroom to speak.

After she closed the door, Uma asked Kalyani, "What's on your mind? Can it be regarding Jack? I have been watching you both all day, how you can't stop looking at each other."

"Is it really that obvious? And yes, it is about me and Jack. I have never told you this, but I have always loved Jack as more than a friend. Our age difference prevented me from approaching Jack emotionally the way I wanted to. Now we are both adults and legally we can be together. It feels right for me to tell you first Uma, because I feel that I can trust you with anything. I am here to ask for your blessing of approval for us to be together as a couple."

"Yes Kalyani, you have my blessing and approval for this and also to get married, if you desire to do so. You both know each other so well from growing up together. It's so beautiful to see two people in love with each other. Watching you smile brought good old memories of my husband when he was still alive. You both made me feel like I was spending a day with my husband again. Thank you for helping me feel alive again, remembering how love makes you feel. This is great news. Now your parents have the chance to choose what will be best for you and not for them."

"Uma, it has been an amazing day for me. To find out that my love from childhood feels the same and that you have approved of our love for each other. This day is the best day of my life. I feel like exploding from the happiness coming from my heart."

Kalyani hugged Uma and said, "Thank you so much for making this day complete. Jack and I no longer have to hide our love for each other."

Uma then said to Kalyani, "I must go right now and talk to Jack, so he can fall asleep with a smile on his face, knowing that your love has been approved by me."

Uma left the guesthouse and walked to the door of Jack and Flower's new house and knocked on the door. Jack opened the door and Uma asked, "Can I speak with you in private?"

Jack said, "Come in and sit down with us in the living room. Whatever you have to say to me can be said in front of my sister, for we have nothing to hide from each other."

Uma looked at Flower and asked her this question, "Have you noticed something special regarding your brother and Kalyani today?"

"Yeah… they both looked like lovebirds that couldn't be separated from each other."

Uma looked at Jack and said, "Don't worry, I have already spoken with Kalyani regarding the love you both have for each other. You both have my approval to get married, if you desire to. I wanted to tell you this tonight so you could both go to sleep and look forward to seeing each other again, knowing that you can show your love in the open instead of hiding it. Love that is expressed in secret can't grow to the fullest. For love to exist is to be seen by others and to make the whole of life better. Can you imagine how beautiful this whole world would be if everyone was in love with someone? I know that you feel released Jack. What about you, Flower? How do you feel?"

"I'm so happy that my brother has someone to love. It's so much easier to fight pain together, than to do it all alone. I must say that I am very happy. For God blessed me to have John to love, and he loves me back like he is my real dad. We all have someone to love, except you, Uma."

"Well, I am older and to be honest, I feel blessed to have all of you to love and my husband left me with good memories to last a lifetime. Jack, tomorrow morning we need to talk about your father's business." Then Uma left Jack and Flower and went back to the guesthouse. When Uma entered the guesthouse, Kalyani was right in Uma's face to ask, "What was Jack's reaction?"

"I did all the talking, while he had a big smile on his face. He told me to tell you that he loves you with all his heart and that he can't wait to be with you again tomorrow."

In that moment Kalyani hugged Uma and said, "Good night and I hope you have a good night sleep."

Uma closed her bedroom door for the night, thanking God for another blessed day.

As usual, Uma was the first one to wake up in the morning.

Filled with expectations for a new day, Uma went to the kitchen and began to make breakfast for everybody. A few minutes later everyone was enjoying breakfast together. While they all sat at the table, Uma brought up a question, "Would anyone like to go fishing?"

They all agreed to go and thought it would be a nice way for everyone to enjoy the day, while getting to know one another better.

Half an hour later, they were on their way. While they walked, Uma approached Jack, "What are your plans regarding your father's business? Your father has a lawyer who handles his paperwork regarding business and family issues. The lawyer's name is Raman and we can call him at any time to come and help us with legal matters regarding family and business. Thanks to Raman, we have a crop to harvest this year. I don't know all details regarding your father's bank account, but Raman does and will tell you all about it. It makes me very pleased to see that you want to continue your father's business."

Uma had a big basket full of treats like sandwiches and fruit. Since the basket was rather heavy to carry, Uma put the basket on Toby's back for him to carry. Uma rewarded Toby in advance by giving him a few bananas.

Along with some blankets, they also brought two fishing rods and tackle, which meant taking turns to fish. The whole walk to the river, Jack and Kalyani held each other's hands and looked happy together. Coming to the river, the men began to fish while the ladies sat down on blankets to see who would be the first one to catch a fish.

John and Jack walked up and down the riverbank and fished next to each other. John asked Jack, "Would you like to see what it takes to pick the harvest?"

"Of course," said Jack, thinking about how Uma had mentioned that John was interested in keeping the family business going. All these years his father had this business and not once had Jack helped pick the harvest, for it had always been the job of the women.

John said to Jack, "I asked this question first, to learn more about this business, and second, to get to know each other more personally."

Jack said, "Do you know how painful it will be for us to do this? Let's inspire each other by seeing which one of us can pick the most baskets."

Jack caught the first fish and gave the fishing rod to his sister for her to try out her luck. John was pleased to catch the second fish and gave his fishing rod to Uma. Then it was Flower's turn to reel in her fish and she gave her fishing rod to Kalyani. Kalyani caught a fish as well and now it was only Uma left to catch a fish. Uma was patient for another half an hour, then was rewarded with a fish as well.

At that moment, they all sat down on blankets by the riverbank and ate lunch together.

"That's great, we are five people and we caught five fish, so we can have a lovely dinner tonight," said Flower.

John said, "I would like to share something that my mother once told me, when I was a young boy. My mother, Susan, once told me this, 'The fish in the ocean is our bread and if we lose them we are dead.'"

After some thought, Flower said, "If we lose all the fish, we still have meat from animals, along with fruit and vegetables to eat. Your mother must refer to something other than fish with this saying."

Uma said, "I know the answer, but I will wait and see if someone else can solve this saying."

After a while Flower said to Uma, "Let us hear the answer. We don't know."

Uma then said, "John's mother was referring to water, because what do we need the most, if not water? If fish die in the water, it means that the water is polluted and we can't drink polluted water. If we do, we will die just like the fish."

John said to Uma, "You are truly a wise woman. It took me a long time to figure out this saying when I was young, and my mother wouldn't give me the answer, either. I had to figure it out myself. It's amazing, the most important thing for our existence is water, yet we abuse it terribly."

After finishing lunch, they decided to walk back home. They needed to prepare for tomorrow's harvest. Before they left, Uma gutted the fish and cleaned it by the river, so the fish would be ready for the grill when they got home. They left the river after having a wonderful time fishing together.

Flower looked at her brother and said, "Would you and Kalyani like to ride Toby's back home?"

"I would love to. What do you say, my love? Would you like to ride Toby with me?"

"Of course, because he is such a nice elephant."

Kalyani and Jack climbed on Toby's back, with Kalyani sitting in the front and Jack behind her. They enjoyed their ride and the beautiful view.

"Thank you, Flower, for letting us ride your elephant. If we hadn't, we may never have seen the beauty of nature like we have seen it today from Toby's back." said Jack.

When they reached the guesthouse, Jack and Kalyani

went to Jack's bedroom to take a nap together. Flower left with Toby to spend some quality time by herself with him in the jungle. Uma and John made a fire together and began to grill the fish they'd caught earlier in the day.

Enjoying each other's company, Uma asked John, "What do you think of Jack?"

"He is a good listener and seems to be a very loving and kind brother to Flower. He doesn't seem to be scared of trying new things and he is very open-minded as well, which shows confidence in himself. One thing for sure, he is very much in love with Kalyani and they look good together. I have a question for you, Uma. How is Jack's faith in God compared with Flower's?"

"Flower was taught to believe in God from the day she could speak. When her speech became more solid, her parents used to say phrases for her to repeat. Phrases like 'God is your strength,' 'God is faithful,' and 'God loves you,' just to mention a few. Flower's faith became very strong at a young age and you can tell because she loves to talk about God to anyone. Jack, on the other hand, was raised without having God in his life until Simon and Sheryl adopted him after his parents' death. When Jack lost his parents in a traffic accident, he became very bitter inside and had a hard time wanting to talk about God.

"Simon told us all to let him be, that God would work on Jack's heart, because at least he was sitting with them and listening when they studied the Word of God together. Slowly but surely, Jack's faith grew stronger. Simon knew that Jack was ready to seek God when Jack came and asked Simon, 'Why does God love me?' Simon told Jack that the answer was found in the Bible. Simon helped Jack to understand more about God, by helping him read about His Son, Jesus, and what He did for us all on the cross. He explained to him why He chose to do it... that there would be no more hope left for mankind to live in love. He became determined to find out why God would love a parentless child.

"As time went by, Jack continued reading the book of love and became more peaceful, as could be seen by the smile on Jack's face. I think the time he spent alone with God in the navy, without any close family members to talk to, has made his faith complete. He has learned to trust in God alone. When he left, all he cared for was himself, but when he came back, his faith had become more mature. Today you can hear when he speaks that he has become a man of faith.

"When I found out about Jack's parents' death and the reason why his heart was bitter, I began to pray for God to restore his heart. It's amazing to see God's hand at work. God not only changed his heart, but he also blessed him with a woman who loves him and knows him for life."

"Oh Uma, I feel so blessed to have come to this place and to have met all of you. I love how you all live by the Word of God and how you all believe in the importance of loving one another. Everywhere I look I see people smiling. I could never dream of a place like this existing in our world. That's why I feel so blessed to be here. You can really feel the presence of God in this place."

Uma then asked John, "Can you go and get the lovebirds?"

"No problem, Uma, I will go and get the lovebirds."

At the same moment, Flower came back with Toby

from their ride in the jungle. Five minutes later, Uma, Flower, John, Jack, and Kalyani were all sitting around the fire, drinking tea and tasting the catch of the day. Everyone was surprised when a man walked up and said, "It looks like you are enjoying yourselves."

With curious eyes, John looked at the man while Uma said, "This is our family lawyer, Raman. I called him to come and explain the paperwork regarding Simon's business. Before we take care of business, please sit down and join us, and relax a little bit before we take on the paperwork. As you can see we are all enjoying the fish we caught earlier today by the river."

Raman said to Uma, "The best tasting fish is the one you catch yourself."

After a while Uma said to Jack, "Why don't you take Raman and John and go talk about your father's business in the guesthouse. Me and the girls will prepare what is needed tomorrow for the harvest.

In the guesthouse Jack said to Raman, "John is part of the family and you can share everthing with him as well."

Raman then said to Jack, "I have something to share regarding your father's will. Simon and I talked about his dreams regarding his business. He hoped that your interest to be part of it would change after you returned from the navy. So, my question to you Jack is are your dreams the same today as when you left for the navy three years ago?"

"I feel sad, Raman, that my father had to die before I changed my mind regarding his business. I hope that you don't look down on me for not being here for my father while he was still alive."

"I would never look down on you, Jack. Sometimes in life we have to face hurdles and go through obstacles in order to change the way we think about things and by doing so, we can see the whole picture. Your father was a man of dreams. He knew the secret of dreams and how to achieve them, yet in all dreams patience is the most important ingredient to have. The bigger the dream, the more patience is needed in order to see our dreams fulfilled. So when Simon and Sheryl came here fifteen years ago and had nothing, they could still see what no one else could see. That there was a better future for this place, but it would take time and patience to make it happen.

"Your parents were called by God to make a difference by being a light for these people, and to show them that nothing is impossible when God's love is in your heart. Simon and Sheryl loved you and Flower more than anything in this world, but I believe in my heart that you already knew that. Simon put money into an account for you and Flower. Money that will help you and Flower start a family someday. It is available to you the day you get married. As it is right now, there is £150,000 in the account for you and Flower to share. If you'd like to get married today Jack, £75,000 is yours to have.

"The second item is regarding your father's business. Like I said, Simon had big dreams for this town and was hoping that his business would expand and grow bigger so that everyone living here could work together who desired to do so. Simon has another ten acres of land that he would like to include in next year's harvest. There is a lot of work needed to prepare this land for harvest. Simon didn't want to start this expansion until he knew that you were onboard with him. Do you still feel like sharing your father's dream by proceeding with this new big task?"

"I would love to, Raman. It will feel like something I helped my father to achieve. To take ten acres of wild land and make it into farmland is not an easy task to take on, but I have lots of faith in the men and women of this town and I know that we can do it together."

"Jack," Raman said, "I believe you can make it happen, because you just said the most important words. I wish that Simon were here right now to hear the words you just said. I am proud of you and I know that Simon would be as well. It makes me happy to be able to go home and to know that you will carry on your father's business. Many people would suffer if you wouldn't. Come here, Jack, I want to give you a hug for giving me release from the worries I had."

Jack then turned to John and said, "My sister speaks very highly of you and says that you want to help us. What kind of experience do you have, John?"

"I went to college in England to become an international business lawyer. In other words, there will be no problem with any paperwork regarding your father's business, which is now your business."

Raman turned to John and asked, "How did you end up in this place?"

"All I can say is that if it weren't for Flower, I wouldn't be alive today. Hearing that, I'm sure you would like to hear the story about how we met. I will let Flower fill in all the details."

After talking business between the three of them for

a while, someone knocked on the door. It was Uma, who said, "Dinner is ready."

They all joined together for dinner and to speak of the next day's plans for the harvest. Uma shared with Raman John's suggestion that everyone experience the picking of the harvest by picking leaves themselves. Even though the picking was typically done by women, John and Jack decided to join in for a full week to see how hard it was to pick it by hand.

Uma said, "I am looking forward to seeing these two men after one day's work in the field. My advice to you both is that tomorrow you listen to what the women in the field tell you, and by doing so, your first day of picking will go so much easier. We will start working at first daylight. Even though it may feel cooler to not wear a hat in the sun, do not be fooled. Wear a hat at all times, or you can easily get sunstroke, which may cripple you for the rest of the week and you will be no good for anyone. I also suggest that since you both have light skin, that you put on sunscreen throughout the day and prevent yourselves from getting burnt by the sun."

After Uma spoke these words, dinner was finished, and everyone went to do their own things. Raman left to go home with a full stomach and a heart full of peace from knowing that Simon was right about his son Jack. His ways would change after being on his own. John and Flower, along with Toby, went for a ride to see the sun set over the harvest fields.

Uma, Jack, and Kalyani were left at the kitchen table.

Jack and Kalyani had spoken to each other earlier about getting married and felt the need to share their feelings about it with Uma. Jack opened his heart to Uma and said, "We both have something very important to share with you Uma. I hope that you don't feel it's too early for Kalyani and I to get married."

With hopeful eyes Jack and Kalyani looked at Uma, not knowing what her answer would be. After looking at them both for a while with a smile on her face, Uma said, "To me it wouldn't matter if you got married with each other a week from now or a year from now. For someone else I would say no, but you both have known each other since childhood. Knowing that you have had feelings for each other as more than just friends, gives me no problem to say yes."

With a relieved heart from receiving the answer that she'd hoped for, Kalyani said to Uma, "We were afraid that you wouldn't agree with marriage this early, but we can't help feeling this way. We were wondering if we could get married at the same time we have our annual celebration after the harvest is finished. That way, we can save money by having one party instead of two."

Uma then said, "I think that is a great idea and I will talk to my sister about this. To give you both peace, I will go and talk to her right now, so that you will have an answer before you go to sleep."

Uma left for her sister's and Jack and Kalyani went for a walk full of anticipation. They wondered what answer Uma would bring back. About one hour later, Uma knocked on the door of the new house, where Jack and Kalyani were waiting to hear what answer Uma received.

Kalyani opened the door and before Uma had a chance to come inside, Kalyani asked Uma, "What did my mother say?"

"Your mother and father both said yes, but with the condition that they are both present at your wedding."

Kalyani said out loud, "Thank you God! I never thought that my mother would approve of me marrying someone I chose."

Uma then said, "This has been a very blessed day. First of all, we went fishing and we all caught a fish, which never happens. Secondly, the lawyer showed up and Jack wants to carry on his father's business. And thirdly, my Jack and Kalyani are getting married. We all have a hard day in front of us tomorrow, so let's go to bed early and get a good night's sleep."

Uma said, "Good night, Flower." Jack and Kalyani went to the guesthouse to join John.

The first words Uma spoke to John were, "Jack and Kalyani want to get married at the harvest party and Kalyani's parents agreed with their marriage. Isn't that great news?"

"It sure is great news! And someone will be smiling all day long tomorrow, no matter what happens."

"This week will surely be hectic, not only do we have a harvest to do, but we also have a wedding to prepare. Tomorrow after work, we must all get together and make a list of things to be done for the wedding," declared Uma.

John said, "Good night," and each person went to his or her own bedroom to go to sleep after having a wonderful day together.

The next morning, as usual, Uma rose at sunrise and began to make breakfast for everyone. John, familiar with the routine, went to get the young ones for breakfast.

When everyone was sitting at the breakfast table, John said, "It is very nice to see you all smiling so early in the morning, especially the ones who are in love. I wish that the whole world could be in love with someone. I remember when my wife, Sarah, and I saw each other in high school for the first time. Love is sometimes hard to understand. Especially when it feels like you belong to each other, yet you know nothing about the person you are looking at for the first time. The first week we admired each other from distance, even when we both knew how we felt about the other.

"When I first saw her that day in high school, I thought Sarah was the most beautiful girl I had ever seen. I was a young rich brat and everyone knew me because of it, but not Sarah, for her parents had just moved into the town where I lived. I guess it was nice to see a fresh face looking at me, seeing me for who I was and not for what I had. It didn't take long for Sarah to see that I was the most popular kid in high school. After a week I approached Sarah. I was afraid of scaring her off, but I still asked her, 'Would you like to go and see a movie together with me? I know that we don't know each other, but I think we can agree that we have are interested in each other.' I thought a movie would be a good way of breaking the ice and getting to know each other better. 'But only if you want to, Sarah.'

"Sarah then says to me, 'How do you know my name? I haven't told you my name.' That had been the easiest thing to find out about her. 'All I had to do was ask one of your classmates.'

"Sarah says to me, 'To be honest with you John, I

have never liked the popular guys in school. Most of them think that they are better than everyone else. But when I look at you John, I can see two faces in one. One face when you are around your buddies and another face when you sit by yourself. I've been watching you... I can see the true you when you're alone, and if I'm right, you are a very lonely person. Everyone thinks that you aren't because they see you as the richest kid in school.' While Sarah was speaking the truth about me and how I felt inside, I couldn't keep the tears from coming down my cheeks.

"The funny thing was that I didn't feel embarrassed to cry in front of Sarah. She made me feel understood for the first time in my life. Then I asked her how she knew my name because I hadn't told her my name. 'Well that's easy, John,' she replied to me. 'Wherever I sit in school I can hear the girls talking about you and saying your name.' Then Sarah finally said the words I had been waiting to hear for what felt like the longest time. 'Yes John, I would love to go and see a movie with you. I just hope it's not a war movie because I don't like to look at those kinds of movies.'

"I told Sarah, 'No, that's not the movie I had in mind. I was hoping that you'd like to see The One Who Flew Over the Cuckoo's Nest. The main character is played by Jack Nicholson.'

"She thought that was a great choice. She'd already seen it once, 'but I would love to see it again with you, because this is a movie you can watch over and over again. It leaves your heart touched about life and how people can be.'

"After that movie we became best friends and we

spent time together every moment we could. Our love kept on growing and we were madly in love with each other. We had not been apart from each other until the day I ran away from the truth that I couldn't make my wife pregnant and have a family. Sarah felt so bad for me and I remember her last words before I left, 'John it will be okay. There are other ways to have children.'

"After leaving Sarah and finding myself, I came to understand that I had always been a spoiled brat who always got what I wanted. I was so selfish that I couldn't see the beauty of adopting a child to be your own. Today I know the truth about my wife. She didn't care how we received a child as long as we could be parents together. Jack, that's where your sister comes in. She can fill the void for me and Sarah by you letting us adopt her. Believe me, I know that we can't replace Simon and Sheryl, but we can do our best to love you and support your needs as a parent does. Looking at you lovebirds reminds me of how much I love my wife and how blessed it makes me feel to have someone loving me back the same way."

Then Jack said to John, "I can't wait to meet your wife. Just as you are a wonderful person, your wife must be as well. But before I give my approval for you to adopt my sister, I need to know your wife in person. I hope that you can understand my concern for my sister."

"Yes I can. I totally agree with you and your request. It's better to know, than to guess, if my wife will be a good mother for Flower."

Then John said, "I don't know why, but I'm very excited to experience picking the harvest by hand."

Everyone finished eating breakfast and left together

to tackle the first day of the harvest. Uma took John under her wings and showed him how to pick tea leaves. She told John, "Remember not to compare yourself with the others. They've all picked tea leaves for the first time, when they started doing it. In everything we do in life, we become better at it the more we do it, so don't worry about speed and how much you can pick, because that is not the reason why you are doing this. You are here for experience and to receive a better understanding of what is involved in Simon's business at harvest time. My advice to you, John, is that during this week of harvest, look around and inhale all the wisdom you can learn and don't get stuck with your head looking down all the time as you pick. If you want to take over where Simon left off, you must do what he did. You must win these peoples' hearts so they will work hard and will always be there for you.

"What you must do is go and talk to everyone while they are picking. Talk to them individually. Ask them questions like, 'How are you doing? How is your family? What kind of dreams do you have? and What do you like to do? These are only a few examples of questions that make people feel recognized and feel that you care about them.

"The reason I say this to you is because it was his way to spend time with his people during the harvest. Then he would know everyone's needs and dreams and what they would like to do. He would give his heart to the people he felt he could help. There was once a boy living in this town and he had a dream of becoming a doctor. His name was Mahesh and Simon became very fond of him. Simon took Mahesh under his wings and taught him how to read and write. When Simon was gone for a business trip, his wife would teach Mahesh. After he learned how to read and write, Simon bought a book about work as a doctor and how to take care of patients. Simon wanted to see if his desires and dreams to be a doctor would change after receiving the knowledge of reading and writing.

"Mahesh's dream to become a doctor meant everything to him, but he couldn't help feeling discouraged by not knowing if he could continue with his education since his parents' budget was limited. Simon was once a child with many dreams and Mahesh reminded him of how it felt when you couldn't make your dreams come through.

"One day Simon went to visit the parents of Mahesh and told them that he would love to pay for their son's education to become a doctor. Simon didn't realize the news he presented to the parents would leave such big impact on the whole family's emotions. They began to shout in thankfulness as they shared tears of joy for knowing that the hope of a better future had come from Simon. Their son, Mahesh, now had an opportunity to make it happen.

"After everyone had collected themselves emotionally, Simon said, 'I will do this the condition that you all will help someone else in need of help when you are able. You, Mahesh, whenever you are home from school, need to be a doctor the best way you can and take care of these people without charging them anything. I will pay for the medicine if they can't afford it. The day you officially become a doctor, you can do whatever you want, but until that day comes, you are an investment to this town.'

"They all hugged each other and Mahesh agreed to do what Simon requested. Today Mahesh lives with his whole family in a house in Goa and has his own clinic. Mahesh was the first child that Simon educated, but he also became the door for Simon's heart to teach so many more children how to read and write. By doing so, many more futures changed direction as their children receive an education.

"Like I said to you before, Simon and his wife had big dreams for this town. I haven't told Jack this yet, but his parents also wanted to build a school for this town. I would like you to talk to Jack about this plan, to build a school, but I was thinking to wait until after the harvest is done. That way Jack won't have too much to deal with at the same time.

"Since Sheryl was a housewife and had some spare time, she wanted to start a school and be the teacher. They both said it was so rewarding to see Mahesh and his family leave this town and to know that they have a good future. Simon always told me that it doesn't take much to change a person's direction for the better, as long as you show them love by putting them before you and loving them through your actions. Time is important for us all, especially our own time. That's why people really feel touched when you sacrifice your own time and give it to someone in need. People will treat you the way you treat them. If you will help people they will help you, but if you don't help people, they will not help you, because they have something to hold against you."

After only two hours of picking the harvest, John's hands and back were sore.

The Family Reunion

John and Uma continued to work and shared stories with each other. Meanwhile, someone entered the town who had never been in it before.

Joshi approached the beautiful blond stranger and asked her, "Who are you looking for?"

"I'm looking for my husband, John Campbell. My name is Sarah Campbell. I was told that I would find him here in this town."

"You sure can find him here. Right now he is picking the harvest with his friends, but I can take you to him if you like. My name is Joshi and it's a pleasure to finally meet you. Your husband John is a great man and he has spoken very highly of you, Sarah."

"Thank you, Joshi, that is very nice to hear. If it is possible, I would like to surprise him and walk up to him by myself, if you could kindly show me where he is."

"I will show you where John is and I will make sure not blow your cover so you can surprise him. Just follow me and we will be there shortly."

Sarah was nervous to see her husband again. It had been six months without hearing his voice or seeing him. Sarah followed Joshi. She looked around and wondered what John was doing in a place like this. She also hoped that John liked her new look.

As the two got closer to the harvest fields, Joshi told Sarah to go and hide behind a tree and he'd be right back. He walked up to Uma and whispered in her ear, "John's wife Sarah just arrived and she wants to surprise John."

Uma told John, "Keep on working, I will be right back."

Joshi walked with Uma to introduce her to Sarah. They walked to the tree where Sarah hid. When Uma reached her, she gave Sarah a welcome hug.

"My heart is so happy to know that John will see his wife again today," Uma said. "I feel like I already know you, for John talks about you a lot, and believe me when I say, that it has only been good."

Uma instructed Sarah on how they would surprise John. She said to Sarah, "I will make sure to keep John's face turned the opposite direction, while you come up behind John and cover his eyes with your hands. I will say, 'Guess who?' to John."

Sarah liked Uma's idea. Uma said, "Wait a couple minutes after I've returned to the field, then approach your husband from behind."

Uma walked back to John and began to work with him again on the opposite side, facing John. He noticed the smile on Uma's face and asked, "Where did this big smile came from?"

Uma said to John, "I'm so happy to see everyone working together as one big happy family." After that answer, John smiled as well, even though he didn't know about the big surprise walking toward him.

At that moment, someone covered his eyes and Uma said to him, "Guess who this is."

John stopped working and tried to think who these female hands belonged to. John's first guess was, "Is it Flower?"

"No John. Why don't you try again?"

"Well, it must be Kalyani then."

"Wrong again," Uma said.

He got desperate and changed his way of thinking. He decided to use his sense of smell and remembered this woman's scent from somewhere. He hadn't smelled this scent in India but somewhere else in the world.

Then it hit him. It must be his wife.

The hands came off his face and John turned around to see that it was his wife Sarah, standing right in front of him. She looked into his eyes for the first time in six months. They hugged each other, weeping out loud, and saying, "I have missed you so much."

They continued to enjoy each other's company for a while. Sarah said to John, "I have never seen you work physically and get dirty while doing it. Look at your hands! They are full of blisters from not being used to this kind of work."

"I know, my love, but it feels great to work alongside these people. They have truly changed my outlook on life and the way you should live it. Look at you Sarah, are you okay? You have lost a lot of weight. I hope I haven't made you sick?"

"Everything will be okay now that we are back together again. After you left me in a rush, I became very depressed with thoughts of us never being together again.

You are everything to me. I am not sick; I just lost my appetite because of missing our love so much. I hope that you still find me attractive."

"Oh Sarah... I am so sorry for all the pain I have caused you. I hope that you will like your new John as well. I am not the same man who left you, but I can say today that I am a better and less selfish husband than I used to be. What I'm trying to say is that the painful months of being alone and tasting death have totally changed the old, spoiled me. I have come to understand the true purpose for living."

"It sounds like you have found the love of God in your heart, John."

"Yes I have, and I feel so alive because of it. I don't think about only myself anymore, but all I can think of is who I can help today. It's a wonderful feeling. I no longer run a race to be better than everyone else, but rather to reach out to people in need, even if they have a hard time asking for help."

"John, I am so happy right now that I can't describe it in words! Let's begin to live together as God wants."

"Sarah, I have made a commitment with that young man over there, Jack, standing next to his wife-to-be, that we are both going to work together this whole harvest to find out how hard this work really is."

Then John said to Uma, "Why don't you and Flower take Sarah and show her around. We will all meet for dinner at the guesthouse when everyone is done working for today."

After Uma, Flower, and Sarah left, Jack and Kalyani joined John to work together.

Jack said to John, "Why don't you go and be with your wife? You haven't seen her for so long."

John replied, "Remember that we both made a promise to each other that we would work the whole harvest together, no matter what happened. Believe me Jack, Sarah and I can wait a couple of hours to be united again, knowing that we both are here and have our whole life in front of us. I bet you have many questions to ask about my wife, but why don't you wait and ask her yourself at the dinner table."

Meanwhile, after Uma and Flower had shown Sarah the town, they all approached the house and the guesthouse.

Sarah stopped walking, looked down toward the town and the harvest fields behind it, and tried to see if she could see her husband. It was too far away to be able to see who was who. She had never seen such a beautiful view of nature before and understood why John loved this place.

Knowing that John was not far away didn't keep Sarah from missing him. The time passed slowly.

Uma and Flower showed Sarah the new house. Then they took Sarah to the guesthouse. When they were done, it was time to cook dinner. Sarah said to Uma, "I would love to surprise John by cooking the dinner because it's been so long since I've cooked for him."

"Of course, Sarah, I loved to cook dinner for my husband as well, when he still was alive. He drowned many years ago, but his love still lives in my heart to this day. He was a wonderful man."

"I am so sorry to hear that, Uma."

"Well, it makes me glad to see that you and John are

back together and you both seem to be very happy. Let's make this dinner special by you cooking it with your love. My plan was to cook chicken and rice along with salad. Do you cook chicken, Sarah?"

"Yes, I do. We love curry chicken. I hope that you have curry I can use."

"Of course, Sarah. You are in India and curry dishes are popular here."

Then Uma showed Sarah where all the spices and food were in the kitchen. Uma asked Sarah, "Would you like to cook dinner outside over an open fire? You could enjoy the first night with your husband watching the sunset and enjoying a good meal at the same time. We enjoy every sunset we can, as long as the weather provides. Today should be a beautiful sunset, since the sky is without clouds."

"That sounds so romantic, Uma. I don't remember the last time John and I watched a sunset together. What a beautiful way to start a new life."

As usual, in the late afternoon, Flower took Toby for a ride in the jungle so he could eat his dinner. Once the fire was going, a metal rack with legs was situated over it. On this rack pots were placed to cook dinner.

"It's so nice to be outside cooking dinner and hearing all the sounds of the jungle at the same time," said Sarah.

Finally the dinner was ready and Sarah could see her husband walking toward her from a distance, with Jack and Kalyani by his side. Uma and Sarah walked to the shed, next to the guesthouse, and took out two folding tables along with eight chairs and set them up not far from the fire. Even though they were only six people for dinner, Uma always set up extra chairs in case someone else showed up.

They placed the tables, along with plates, glasses, forks, knives, and the food, on the tables. John walked up behind his wife and whispered in her ear, "The food smells so good, darling."

Sarah turned around and hugged her husband. She looked into his eyes and said, "I am so happy that we are back together again."

"Me too. I was scared that you had given up on me. Let me go wash my hands and then we can enjoy this good dinner and afterward we can all share stories."

Flower and Toby also arrived for dinner.

When everyone was sitting around the table Uma said, "Guess who cooked the dinner tonight?"

John was the first one to guess, as he looked at his wife's smiling face. "It is pretty obvious that it must have been Sarah, with that big smile on her face."

Uma replied to John, "You are right. I must say that your wife is a good cook."

Through the whole dinner, John and Sarah couldn't take their eyes off each other. They even shed tears of joy for being back together. After cleaning up dinner, they all sat down around the fireplace to continue their night by sharing stories.

Flower asked a question of John, "Why do you love your wife so much?"

"The list is very long, since she has many good qualities. But let me share the quality that I love, which is also rare among people these days. She has an ability to look beyond the problem and understand why the situation appeared in the first place. When I found out the truth about myself, I became so angry and ashamed that all I wanted to do was to run away, instead of facing the truth. I should have been calm and apologized to my wife for accusing and blaming her, but I allowed my anger to control my actions. I knew that Sarah would understand where my anger was coming from, which gave me the strength to not give up on our love. Today I am glad that I didn't, for I know in my heart that Sarah will love her new husband even more. The rest of her strengths you will see as you spend time with her."

Jack turned to Sarah, "What kind of work do you do in England?"

"I'm a housewife. I keep the house clean and take care of my husband's needs."

Jack said, "That was the same with my mother, Sheryl. She was also a housewife like you, and her job was to take care of me and Flower as well." Then Jacked asked, "What kind of education you have?"

She answered, "I went to high school, where I met John. After high school, I did two years of college in Social Studies."

"I know that you just came here Sarah, but for some reason I feel that you might be interested to follow up what my mother was about to start in this town. My parents passed away in a fire about a year ago. They had a dream to make this town into a better place by building a school and providing an education in order to give these people an opportunity to reach a better future."

"I'm sorry, Uma," John said, cutting into the conversation, "but I couldn't hold our secret after seeing my wife.

I told Jack about the plans to build a school on the way back from the field for dinner."

Everyone looked at Sarah to see her reaction.

She answered back with excitement, "Well I have never been a teacher, but I remember how I was taught to read and write and I guess all I have to do is to use the same way to teach these people. If my husband approached me to do this task, I would gladly do it. To be honest, I don't care what I do as long as I can be with my husband."

Jack then said, "We have a dilemma among us when it comes to speaking English. Some people here speak English, but most of them speak only their native language."

Uma answered back, "We could have more than one class if we have more than one teacher. The children that already speak English could learn how to read and write from Sarah. The ones that need to learn to speak English can learn from Uma and Kalyani."

Jack looked at Uma and said, "That it is a great idea. By the way, it is not a secret regarding the school and expanding my father's business. Before I left for the navy my father shared his dreams with me and told me that it would mean a lot to him, if I would like to be part of it. That is why he told me before I left. He said, 'Don't give me an answer now, but when you come back.' I wish I'd told him back then, but I wasn't sure what I wanted with my life. My father has ten acres to be harvested this week.

"After the tea harvest is done we have ten more acres of wild land to prepare for the tea plants. We could keep two acres for building a school. My father also had a plan for all those who were working for him. I feel the need to speak to our people so that everyone can be involved with building the school, so that they can each feel rewarded by being part of it. Do we all agree with my parents' dream about this town and its people? I need all of your help to make this happen."

Everyone came to an agreement and became excited to continue Simon and Sheryl's plans for the town.

Uma said, "We have lots of great work ahead of us. We need to sit down again and discuss our options. How can we make all of this happen in a way that is best for everyone? How can we make this town grow stronger in knowledge and therefore be able to open new doors of life to many? Let's concentrate on the blessings that God has given us today.

"The blessing to see the love of John and Sarah bloom again and how much richer it has become than before when they were both apart from each other. Also the blessing that we can all harvest together as a family in God, with our hearts filled with His love and a bright future, as we allow God to guide our steps and bring glory to His name."

Then, from out of nowhere, Toby filled his trunk with water from the garden barrel and began to spray water on everyone's faces over and over again. Flower laughed and said, "I guess it's hard to keep all your love and happiness inside, even if you're an elephant. We all express ourselves differently when we are happy. This is how Toby is expressing his happiness, so please don't be mad at him, after all, it's only water."

"How can I be mad when it feels like I have been so

blessed," said John, "For never in my life could I dream that an elephant would share his love with me by soaking me in water."

Sarah asked Flower, "Why is there only one elephant in the whole town? My husband told me all about you in his letter, but he didn't tell me why an elephant would follow you like a magnet."

"We rescued each other from death at the same time and we have become as one because of it. God saved my life on that terrible day by bringing Toby into my life. He has protected me from wild animals of the jungle while we lived in it for almost a year." And in the honesty typical of all children, Flower said to Sarah, "I would love to be adopted by you and John and to be your daughter. You must know one thing, though. I am not going anywhere without my elephant and I hope you understand why."

John smiled and said, "Oh now, there will be no problem with that issue. Toby is part of the family and where we go, he will also go."

Then John asked Sarah, "What would you like to do tomorrow?"

"She needs to rest tomorrow after her long journey here," said Uma. "She can walk around with Flower and maybe go for a ride with Toby. I think it would be a great way for them to get to know each other better. After all, children should know their parents."

Sarah replied, "To be honest, I would love to be with my husband in the field tomorrow, but my heart desires more to get to know my daughter-to-be. Plus, I have never ridden an elephant before. And now, I would like to retire for the night and be alone with my husband before going to sleep."

Uma said, "That is a great idea for us all. I'm sure that we all are tired after a long day of work."

Jack, Kalyani and Flower went to sleep in the new house, and Uma, John and Sarah went to their bedrooms in the guesthouse.

Sarah was the most tired of them all from a long journey and a day full of excitement, being reunited with her husband. They lay in the bed with her head resting on his chest. They enjoyed this moment of being together again. No words were spoken to each other for a while, as they contented themselves with inhaling the truth. The day they had both been waiting for had finally come, the beginning of life together again with a clean slate and a new beginning having a family together.

With a heart full of happiness and thankfulness, Sarah shed a tear onto John's chest. John felt the wetness from her tear and with deep concern asked "Sarah, are you okay?"

Sarah lifted her head and looked into the eyes of her husband and said, "Oh, John, I am so happy that we are back together. My love, believe me when I say, they are not tears of sadness but of joy. The days we've been apart have tormented me severely. I've been surrounded by people who love and care for me, but they cannot fill my need to be with the one I love with all my heart. You.

"Just like you, I have truly been seeking God for answers regarding love and why it's so important to us all. I have learned that love is what you want it to be, that what you believe guides your heart's emotions and they become your actions."

Sarah continued "In every relationship you must seek the deepest understanding. Sometimes the truth is painful to accept right away, but to be honest with you John, because of this time being without you, I have come to understand how much you mean to me. Yes, the first two weeks after you left, I was really angry with you. I was thinking 'How can he leave me? What have I done wrong? He better come back or else,' and many more thoughts. I waited to receive an answer regarding the situation we were both in.

"As time went by, new thoughts entered my head. Thoughts like, 'Maybe he doesn't love me anymore. Has he found someone else? All these years we've been together for what?' and of course, the thought, 'See if you can find a better women than me.' God showed me the truth regarding my angry feelings. Most of the time when we act out in anger we make the wrong choice. I am also happy to see that you are the same John I fell in love with, but at the same time, you are so different. We have been through many painful days apart from each other and I know that it's changed me for the better. And by looking at you, I must say that I like the way you've turned out as well."

John said, "Isn't it great that God has given us a clean slate with which to start all over again? He knew that we would both become better and stronger in love because of what we would go through while being apart. Oh Sarah, today I feel so much richer in life, because I can say that I've been blessed with true love. We have received the love of God in our hearts, and because of His love, we didn't give up on each other. Instead He taught us that love doesn't give up but always fights to stay alive."

After those words, they hugged and shared tears of joy. They slowly fell asleep knowing that tomorrow would be another day and a future they'd been longing to share with each other again.

Early the next morning, just before sunrise, Sarah woke up and looked at John sleeping with a heart full of happiness. She knew that she was not dreaming of lying beside her husband. Sarah thought, "I hope I can make it out of the bed without waking him up. I'd love to surprise my love with breakfast in bed."

Slowly and gently, Sarah got out of bed without waking John. She went to the kitchen to prepare breakfast for her husband. Luckily, at the same moment, Uma entered the kitchen and helped Sarah find the things needed for breakfast and to help her surprise John.

Sarah asked Uma, "Do you have any eggs? I would like to make an omelet for John."

Uma answered back and said, "I hope four eggs is enough. That's all we have left."

"That's funny Uma. A four-egg omelet is what I used to make John for breakfast at home."

"Take them, Sarah, and make the best omelet ever for him. No matter what, I know that John will enjoy eating it, with you at his side."

Sarah made the omelet along with tea and some fruit and brought it to John, while Uma made breakfast for everyone else.

Sarah admired her husband from distance while he slept.

John's eyes slowly opened and connected with Sarah's and he said to her, "Oh, thank God that you are real and not a dream. This is with no doubt the most beautiful morning of my life. I get to wake up and see my wife smiling at me, with a new blooming love in her heart. And to top it off, she brings me an omelet, which I haven't had since I was home! Please Sarah, put the tray on the floor and come hug me."

A moment later John finished his omelet and walked out of the bedroom with his wife. They joined Uma in the kitchen with the rest of the family. John watched everyone eat their breakfast and said, "It is so nice to enjoy breakfast with your loved ones right next to you. To see everyone smiling out of happiness for each other."

Jack said, "I'm so happy that you and your wife are back together again, John. But to be honest, I have one problem with it."

Everyone stopped smiling and wondered what Jack meant with these serious words. Jack looked at John and said, "I cannot accept another day of work from you with your wife here. I don't know about you John, but I don't need another day of work in the field to understand how hard the work is. I think it's more important for you and Sarah to enjoy each other again."

Uma spoke up next and said, "I'm glad that we are on the same page, Jack. We all have many things to do regarding a wedding that is waiting to be planned and organized. We will never have the time to make it happen if we are all picking the harvest this year. There are plenty of workers to get it done. We need to prepare for the wedding, starting today. I believe we are all in need of clothing, for we all want to look our best on Jack and Kalyani's wedding six days from now."

Sarah cut in and said, "I would love to help arrange the wedding with Kalyani and Uma, because I have arranged many weddings in England."

Uma, relieved, said, "Oh Sarah! You don't know how much those words lift my stress. To be honest, I have never planned a wedding before, so you must understand how blessed I feel. It's so good to know that you are experienced with weddings."

Sarah looked at Uma and Kalyani and said, "Believe me, girls, we will have so much fun making this wedding complete and beautiful."

Uma said, "There is very little time left to make it happen. The day of the harvest party is around the corner and I must be honest, shortcuts have to be made in order for us to have the wedding at the same time.

John cut into the conversation and said, "I accept your suggestion Jack. Sarah and I were sharing some thoughts on the wedding last night before we fell asleep. We can make the wedding happen on time with the condition that you all allow us to pay for everyone's clothing for the wedding.

"Today we must go to the city where the family doctor lives. When I was there with Flower, I saw a clothing store where they custom-make clothing for weddings. They provide all of the necessary things to complete a wedding. If we all go there today, the store can measure our sizes. There is a possibility that we can make the wedding happen on time. We can even help decide how the wedding will look regarding flowers, food, plates, silverware, table cloths, and so on.

"I hope you will all accept my invitation to provide for whatever is necessary for the wedding, by allowing me to be a father of provision for Jack and Kalyani's wedding. By doing so you will give me a chance to return to you the friendship you have given me, one filled with a kind of love I have never experienced before. You took me in and accepted me just as I was. That kind of love doesn't exist everywhere in the world, but I was blessed to find it here. You can't buy this kind of love."

At that moment Flower began to jump up and down in excitement and said, "I get to wear a beautiful dress again!"

Everyone looked at Flower's reaction and John asked, "Do you agree with this proposal?"

After everyone agreed, Uma told John, "The family lawyer called last night and told me that your passport is ready to be picked up."

John replied to Uma, "Is God's timing perfect or what? Since the passport is ready, I can now open a bank account to transfer money and pay the doctor."

John walked up and hugged Uma and said to her, "This turned out to be a great beginning of a new day."

Uma then said to John, "I will go right now to see if Joshi can drive us all to the city in the bus he owns."

After Uma left, everyone finished their breakfast and went to get ready for the trip. Half an hour later, everyone was waiting outside. Uma pulled up with the bus along with Joshi. Uma stepped out from the bus and said to everyone, "God must want for this day to be complete. When I came to Joshi, he had just finished changing the oil in the bus and said to me, 'I can take you wherever you need to go.'"

Excitedly Uma said, "Come on, jump into the bus so the journey can begin." Everyone sat on the bus except Uma and Flower, who stood outside the bus having a conversation regarding Toby and who was going to take care of him while everyone was in the city.

Uma said to everyone, "I will stay behind and take care of Toby. I want to wear my wedding dress from my wedding day. It would mean a lot to wear it again and by doing so I will honor the love in my heart for my husband again."

Before they left, Uma said, while looking at Sarah, "It's a beautiful dress and I know you will like it."

Sarah asked Uma, "What the color is the dress?"

"The dress is light blue."

Sarah then looked at Kalyani and said, "I know that it is your wedding, but I must ask you a personal question. Would you mind wearing a light blue wedding dress at your wedding?"

"I wouldn't mind at all. I like that color and it would be an honor for me to wear the same color as Uma. She has done so much for me."

"That's great," Flower replied. "I have a light blue dress as well, that the doctor gave me when John and I went to the city last time."

The bus left after everyone said goodbye to Uma, and the journey to the big city began. Sarah sat with Kalyani and John sat beside Jack so they could spend the drive to the city getting to know each other even more. Kalyani looked at Sarah and asked, "Can you be my maid of honor?"

Sarah answered, "I would love to, Kalyani. Thank you for asking me."

Then Kalyani told Sarah her situation. "Uma and my mother are sisters, and thank God that Uma agrees with me regarding forced love in a marriage. That's why I am living with Uma and my hope is that my parents will change their attitude after I get married to Jack."

"I believe there is a big chance for your parents to come around and receive you with a new heart after this wedding is over. You would be surprised, Kalyani, how many people I've seen change their ways at weddings. I don't believe that people change other people at a wedding, but rather, what a wedding stands for is what changes them. A wedding is the ultimate goal of life. Finding a partner for life and knowing in your heart that the person you are getting married with will be by your side for the rest of your life is the best gift.

"The bottom line is that it's a big blessing to get married. A marriage only happens when both partners of a relationship agree upon it. Strength in true love is not about being perfect, but to act rightly when troubles, hardships, and disappointments enter the relationship and try to destroy the love between two people who truly love each other."

"Those are well spoken words of wisdom, Sarah, and it's not hard to understand why John loves you so much."

At that moment Jack turned to John and asked him, "John, would you mind being the best man at my wedding? It would mean a lot to me, since I know how Flower feels about you. And to be honest, I like you a lot as well."

"Thank you so much Jack. I never imagined that you'd ask me for such an honorable task, and yes, I would love to be your best man at the wedding."

Jack then looked at John and said, "Oh, what a big relief! If you didn't accept my offer, to be honest, there isn't anyone else I want in the best man's shoes at my wedding. You are the closest friend that I have."

"Once again, thank you so much Jack. It means a lot to me to be able to be your friend and best man."

Jack then asked John, "What is the first thing to do when we arrive in the city?"

John turned to his wife and said, "Sarah, you are in charge of planning the wedding, so what's first on the list to do when we arrive?"

Sarah looked at John and said, "What was the name of the store that can help us with the wedding?"

"The store wasn't far away from the doctor's clinic, and its name was easy to remember because it was called, 'All You Need for A Wedding.'"

Sarah said, "The first thing we should do is to go to this store. I have a credit card with me, so I can pay a deposit toward the bill. After our clothes have been measured, we all need to agree upon a solution for all of the plates and glasses for the wedding. It would be very expensive to supply dishes for everyone when talking about plates, glasses, forks, knives, spoons, etcetera. There will be close to one hundred people attending this wedding.

"I have a suggestion. Today there will likely be beautiful one-time-use paper plates that we should get to use as dinner plates. A wedding is not remembered by what you ate your food on, but rather the people who came and celebrated your love. After all is said and done, everyone attending a wedding is there because they believe what it stands for: LOVE."

Kalyani looked at Jack and said, "I agree with Sarah. You get married for love and not for a fancy show."

Jack looked at Kalyani and said, "Whatever my wife-to-be says, I agree with her completely. I know that I will not love her less if I drink wine from a plastic cup instead of a crystal glass, for love is not found in a glass, but in your heart."

"I am very glad," Sarah replied. "You feeling the same way makes the wedding planning much easier. Next on the list are the flowers, for there must be flowers at a wedding, and lots of them, to make the wedding beautiful."

To Sarah's amazement, Flower spoke up and said, "I'm so glad that I can help at the wedding. Leave the flower arrangement job to me, Sarah. I promise you will not be disappointed."

Before Sarah had a chance to disapprove of Flower's request, John looked at Sarah and said, "My love, you have no idea how Flower can transform flowers into beauty with her hands. I wish I could take you to the old abandoned temple in the jungle, so that you could see, for its beauty would speak for itself."

Flower spoke up and said, "Sarah, you have no idea what kind of beautiful flowers the jungle offers. The good thing is that they are all for free, as is my labor. It will be my wedding gift for Jack and Kalyani."

Sarah said, "This is without a doubt the most interesting, and at the same time, the easiest wedding I have ever planned for anyone. I cannot wait to see what you can make out of flowers, my dear Flower girl."

Sarah traded her seat with Jack and sat down next

to her husband to talk of personal planning. "Regarding money, what are your plans?"

"When I was in the city with the doctor, he showed me a bank I could use to arrange all that I needed regarding finances. Since my passport is done, my plan was to go and get the passport, then go to the bank and open an account and transfer money from England into it. This way we have money toward whatever we need. After this is done, we need to go to the agency regarding the adoption of Flower to be our daughter. I couldn't file the papers last time because I didn't have any identification, and I thought it would be better if we did it together in person anyway."

Sarah said, "We are both very blessed to be able to adopt a girl like Flower. I hope the paperwork won't take too long. I am hoping to go back to England and be a support to my brother's pregnant wife."

"Oh Sarah, even if the papers are not done in time, we will still make it back in time for the baby's delivery. I can't wait to take a trip back home and see my whole family as a new man. I am sure that Flower is very eager to meet all our family members as well."

At noontime, Joshi pulled up in front of the store. Everyone got out, except Joshi, who went to park the bus. Before everyone entered the store, Sarah shared some words of advice, "When we get inside, John and Jack are the ones to be measured first. This way they can leave with Joshi and take care of other business, while we girls shop for things we'd like for the wedding. When the men return, I am hoping that the only thing we'll have left to do, before going home, is for us to go to the adoption agency."

Everyone entered the store and were greeted by the owners, who were a middle-aged couple from England. Sarah opened the conversation and said to the owner of the store, "We are preparing for a wedding that will happen less than six days from now. Can you help us?"

The lady of the store answered, "To be honest with you, my husband and I have never planned a wedding with such short notice. But, it must be your lucky day because we are not too busy right now. I have one concern. Are you planning to wear your own clothes or do you need clothes for the wedding?"

"I brought this dress to show you and see if you might have the same color to offer. If you can, there will be only two dresses to make."

The lady introduced herself, "My name is Karen and my husband's name is Mike." Karen took the dress and said to Sarah, "Let me go in the back and see if your luck is holding up."

After a few minutes Karen returned and delivered good news and said, "Look, it's the same color and I have enough to make two dresses. I will have to work extra hours to have them done in time, so it will cost you little more since time is very limited."

John cut in and said, "Money is no issue and I will personally pay you extra for your sacrifice to make it happen."

Karen then looked at the men and said, "What about you? Do you need clothes as well?"

John replied, "I am the best man and Jack next to me is the groom. We need suits."

"Sir, what color would you like?"

"I was thinking about dark blue, since the girls will

wear light blue dresses. I think it will be a nice contrast from light to dark in the same color," said Jack.

Sarah then asked Karen, "Can you take the measurements of these two men so they can go take care of other business? We girls will continue the planning of the wedding."

Karen took the measurements of John and Jack and they both left to go to the English Embassy, along with Joshi, who was waiting outside the store.

A couple of hours later, Jack and John entered the wedding store again, after picking up John's passport and going to the bank.

Sarah and Karen were nearly done. All that was left to do was the paperwork and settling the bill. After thanking Karen and Mike for all of their help, everyone left the store and went to take care of the last thing on the list before going back home: filing for the adoption of Flower.

Twenty minutes later, the bus arrived at the adoption office. Jack and his sister, along with John and Sarah, entered the building. Everyone involved in Flower's adoption were in attendance at the adoption agency at the same time, which helped to speed up all the paperwork. One hour later, everyone walked outside to rejoin the others who waited on the bus.

Before leaving the city to go home, they stopped at the outskirt of the city for a bit of food, since everyone was starving and the journey back home would last a few hours. After they finished eating at a nice restaurant, everyone was eager to jump back into the bus to continue the trip back home. Not many words were spoken on the way home because of full stomachs and being tired after a hectic day. A few minutes into the trip, everyone was asleep, except the driver, in the comfortable seats of the bus. The journey back home was driven in the dark of the night. Everyone woke up at home when Joshi slammed the bus door. Uma was outside with Toby to greet them.

The first one out of the bus was Flower. She gave her elephant a hug and thanked Uma for taking care of him. Once everyone was outside, Uma said "Come and join me at the guesthouse and tell me how things went today in the city. I also have some news to share."

A few minutes later, sitting in the guesthouse, Uma said, "Well, I have great news from the police. They came by this morning because they captured those men who killed Simon and Sheryl. They were robbing a gas station and the police happened to be nearby. With Flower's pictures they were able to get them to confess to the murders. Now we can all sleep better. They will be in prison for life. Now, tell me about your day."

Sarah said to Uma, "It has been a very successful day. I can't believe all the things we got done in one day."

After sharing about the wedding and its plans, Sarah also shared with Uma, "The good news is that all of the paperwork is done for the adoption of Flower. All we can do now is wait to hear what they say. This can take up to sixty days to find out.

"On the journey to the city I found out that Flower has a hidden talent when it comes to arranging flowers. I heard that she is very good at it and have been informed that the proof is located at an old temple in the jungle.

"So, Uma, I was hoping that Flower, John and myself could go to this place tomorrow. I am dying to see what

Flower can do with flowers. I hope there is nothing tomorrow to hinder us from going to this place."

"No, Sarah, you are all free to go and enjoy a wonderful elephant ride to this temple. I did it and I must say that it was a wonderful experience to sit high above the ground on the back of an elephant through the wild jungle."

Those were the last words of the night and another day had gone by with many new good memories. They all went to sleep for the night. Being full of good anticipation and eager to experience something that she'd never experienced before, Sarah was the first one to wake up. She jumped out of bed to get cleaned up in the bathroom and went to make breakfast for everyone.

Uma woke up hearing someone in the kitchen and joined Sarah to help her make breakfast. Uma was pleased to see Sarah awake so early and asked her, "Have you always been an early bird? You are even singing."

"Yes, my favorite time of the day is when I wake up and realize that God has given me another blessed day to make a difference in the way I treat people. And to be honest with you Uma, I'm still giddy with all of the happiness in my heart for being together again with the man who means everything to me. Such a burden has left me knowing that I can go and see my husband anytime I want, instead of wondering if I will ever see him again. I don't know about you, but to me, life is complete when you have someone to love and when they love you back as well. Then you grow older and become more and more as one."

"I know what you are talking about, Sarah. When I look at you and John together, I can't help but think about how my loving husband left me because of a stupid drowning accident. Don't worry, time has allowed me to live without him. Because of it, I realize how much our love for each other meant. I can't imagine someone else in my life to take his place, and I am getting older anyway.

"But I'm very happy to have all you nice people in my life as my friends. You are all a family I have never had the opportunity to have myself. I am so happy, Sarah, that John met Flower in the jungle and that they both took a liking to each other. Now you as a loving wife have been blessed with a family, as you and John adopt Flower as your own child, and take Jack under your wings.

"It's so beautiful to see that someone else can fill another's void of family. The only way it can be done is for the adoption to be made in love. My heart is overwhelmed with peace from knowing that the two people who are about to adopt Flower are truly loving people, and will take good care of a little girl whom I love more than anything."

After Uma spoke, John entered the kitchen and asked, "Would you like me to go get everyone for breakfast?"

Uma answered, "Let the kids sleep a little longer. Breakfast is not ready yet and what you see is the food you will take on your journey into the jungle today."

John walked up to his wife and hugged her good morning. He said, "My love, this day will be a day to remember. I know that you will enjoy what you are about to experience today in the jungle."

"You are so right, John. I had a hard time sleeping last night. I kept thinking about going into the wild jungle and not knowing what to expect has made me a little nervous, but it's a good nervousness. Today, since it's the first time we'll be alone with Flower, we can begin bonding as a family."

Uma looked at Sarah and said, "It will be a complete day of quality time for you as a family."

"The ride there takes a few hours. After that you will spend some time together at the temple, then you have a few hours ride back home. My guess is that you will be back today when there is not much sunlight left. By the looks of it, I say that we will have a beautiful and sunny day to enjoy."

Uma packed the food for the journey into a basket and then told John, "Can you go and wake up the young ones at the new house?"

John opened the door leading into the house and was surprised to see Kalyani, Jack and Flower already up and ready to face a new day together as a complete family. Flower ran up to John, hugged him, and said, "Good morning."

John said, "Good morning! Breakfast is ready. It's going to be a beautiful day for each one of us to enjoy."

They all went back to the guesthouse to join Uma and Sarah at the breakfast table. While they ate breakfast, Jack asked Sarah, "How do you like it here so far?"

"I must admit that this place is very laid back, and it has its own kind of peace that I haven't experienced before, and I've been to lots of places in the world with my husband."

Jack replied, "I know exactly what you mean regarding the special peace this place has. The funny thing is that I realized it after being away in the navy. When I came back home, I came to understand that all along it was this place that my heart had been longing for. This town is all I need and I feel rich being here among these people. They are all honest and sincere. Today I know and understand why there is so much peace in this little village."

Sarah said, "I feel sad that I can't see and speak with Simon and Sheryl in person. But when I look at you and Flower and how you both are as individuals, I understand that they must have loved you very much. I can tell that they made a good impact on you, to also believe in love and how it affects all who have it in their lives. Love is amazing, Jack, and I have learned a lot about how it can change people from being selfish to more loving toward others. You can't buy love. True love is a commitment between two people and it only grows stronger when both sides of the relationship are in it for a lifetime.

"Unfortunately, many people aren't willing to commit themselves to each other for life through marriage, for the world and its morals have changed. But the truth about the importance of love will never change, for without love, how can anyone be happy?"

"Thanks, Sarah, for making a new day so special by sharing such nice words about my parents and love. Your words truly touched my heart and made me realize how blessed I've been to have parents like them to guide me in the right direction. Flower mentioned that she is taking you and John on a ride with Toby to the temple in the jungle. Believe me, you will love what you are about to experience today. It is such a nice view."

"That's what everyone has been telling me. I never

thought that I would ride on an elephant's back through a wild jungle, so I must say that I'm a little bit nervous. I am also very excited to see it all."

"I like you a lot, Sarah. I must be honest and say that I will miss you today while we pick the harvest, knowing that you will see the beautiful temple my sister transformed. I haven't yet seen it myself."

"Thank you, Jack. I like you a lot as well. I'll be sure to share my experiences with you when I come back tonight."

After everyone finished eating breakfast, Uma, Kalyani, and Jack said goodbye to John, Flower, and Sarah who started their journey to the temple on Toby's back. Two hours later, Flower came across something she had hoped to never see: a poacher's trap.

Flower told Toby, "Stop walking," as he was standing right next to the trap. "Look John, my father told me about these kinds of hunters of wild animals, so-called poachers, which only hunt to get what's valuable in the black market, like animal skins and elephant tusks. This trap is made for a tiger."

Flower then said to herself, "Thank God it's already been used. It's wide open and deserted."

"Poachers dig a big hole in the ground about two meters by two meters wide and about two and a half meters deep. Then they cover the hole with branches and leaves to match the ground and blend it with its surroundings. Before covering the hole, live bait, like a goat for example, is put in the hole to draw a tiger to it, since a tiger hunts for live prey. Other animals, like elephants, fall into these traps. Once a tiger or an elephant falls into the deep hole, it's trapped and unable to get out. This way the animal is alive when the hunter comes for it and can skin the tiger fresh," explained Flower.

"Seeing this troubles me, John. I have never seen poacher traps in this part of the jungle before. I sure don't want to lose Toby in one of these traps by mistake, which means I must be careful to keep him close to my sight. When we return to town we must report what we've seen to the jungle rangers, and let them know what is going on in our area, which has tigers."

Sarah said to Flower, "It's sad but true, there have always been and always will be people in this world who care more about money than for others. Money is their love. Money is the root of all evil, the more you have the more you want. In other words, you are never satisfied with what you have but always hunger for more. The good thing is that we are not these kind of people and as long as any of us are with Toby, nothing bad can happen to him without us knowing it."

"Thank you, Sarah. I couldn't help but worry about Toby's well-being after seeing this trap, but you are right, as long as one of us is with Toby, nothing bad can happen to him. This brings peace to my heart again."

After staring at the empty trap for a bit, they continued their journey to the temple. They could see the walls of the temple from a distance. At that same moment, John said, "I don't know about you, but I am very hungry and I can't wait to get inside the temple to enjoy the good sandwiches that Uma made for us."

A few minutes later they entered the temple courts and nothing had changed except that the monkeys were back and had made a mess again. They all stood on the floor of the temple court when Flower looked at John and said to him, "I am sorry John, but I will not fix this place again; the monkeys can be here if they want to."

Flower then looked at Sarah and said, "I am sorry that you can't see it the way I would like you to see this place, but I am sure that John can tell how this place once looked. At least this time the monkeys left the orchids in the tree."

"So this is the beautiful temple where you and Toby lived for almost a year. Mess or not, Flower, I can see that you have done a wonderful job fixing this place up to make it a loveable place for you and Toby. John was not mistaken when he told me that you have been blessed with a special gift with flowers. You make them look truly alive and beautiful by mixing together all of their colors."

They all sat down to enjoy the picnic lunch together, imagining how it once looked before being destroyed by the monkeys. After admiring the temple and enjoying the food, John said, "A man's actions become another man's emotions, and that man's emotions become another man's despair. I can imagine how beautiful this temple used to be, in its original shape, until someone came and wrecked it. One man's disagreement destroyed it. Every action leads to a reaction and with every reaction there's a consequence.

"How many times in history has war occurred because someone didn't agree with another person or wanted something that someone else had. Look at me, for example. Why did I run away from my wife when I realized that we couldn't have our own child? Was it because of the news I heard or was it because of my own emotions boiling up inside of me due to the disappointment of not being able to have what I wanted to have? Instead of accepting the circumstances, we act on how we feel about the circumstances.

"The truth isn't based on how we feel, but on accepting the situation regardless of the emotions that boil up within you. Accepting something that you cannot change brings peace to your heart instead of despair. That's why my heart is so grateful today. My wife didn't leave me because of the poor judgment of my emotions, but she stayed knowing that we can all act wrongly when we let our emotions take over.

"My wife knows my personality being her husband, and personality is not being based on emotion, but rather how you act from your heart."

Sarah walked over to her husband and said to him, "Oh John, come here. I want to give you a hug after hearing such beautiful words from the loving heart that I fell in love with many years ago."

While John and Sarah hugged, Sarah looked at him and said, "I love you so much. God has really blessed us both during this time apart. Because of what we've gone through, we can see more clearly and understand what we have together as a husband and wife. We have a love that doesn't give up, which means that we have been blessed with true love."

"I couldn't have said it better myself, Sarah. Not only do we know how strong our love is for each other, but we have been blessed with these people coming into our lives and giving us the opportunity we've both been waiting for, to be parents of a child."

Sarah turned to Flower and said, "Thank you so much for showing me your favorite place and sharing with me the beauty of it. Even if I can't see the completeness of the work of your hands, my mind can, and this temple is really beautiful, Flower."

"Thank you. Those words means a lot to me. I'm so happy to be blessed as well, to have new parents who love me dearly. I don't know about you, but I miss my brother Jack and would like to spend some time with him. We've been apart so long. Would you mind if we go back home? You have now seen what I wanted to show you."

"Yes Flower, I'm ready to go back to town to mingle and get to know everyone better." They began their journey back home.

Meanwhile, while working in the harvest field, Kalyani and Uma talked about their new and old friends coming into their lives. Jack was deep in thought about love and what an impact everyone had made on each other, especially in regard to John and Sarah. After thinking to himself for a while, he shared these his thoughts with Uma and said, "Isn't love beautiful? How it opens new doors and closes old ones? Especially if you're willing to receive love that's been given to you through someone who wasn't part of the family from the beginning.

"I have one question for you, Uma, regarding love. What is more beautiful, to give love or to receive love from someone you don't know?"

"My dear Jack, that is a deep question but I will answer it by the way I see it. Since we talked about John and Sarah, I will make an example regarding them. Would the whole town have greeted John with open arms, the way we all did, if he had come on his own, without Flower? No one would have had anything by which to judge him. Would we all have accepted him so quickly if we hadn't known what Flower had been through with the loss of her parents? Compassion springs up toward someone and their situation when you can feel yourself in their situation. We can all imagine the feeling of losing our parents the way Flower lost hers.

"John entering into Flower's life was not planned by man, but by God. So my answer to your question is that I feel it is more beautiful to receive love than to give love, because without receiving God's love into our hearts, how can we begin to learn how to love like He does? After all, isn't a person's love displayed through the actions he first believed from within his heart? The Bible teaches us in John 1:12, 'Yet to all who received Him, to those who believed in His name, He gave the right to become children of God.'

"Just like John was received with love from all of us, by accepting him to be a father for Flower, so also our God in heaven wants to be a Father for us all. But the first step is to receive Him into your life through faith and believe that He rewards those who earnestly seek Him. Once His love dwells in your heart, it becomes more blessed to give love than to receive love, for His love can give life to others, if you are willing to receive Him into your heart."

Uma continued with these words, "Look at the whole picture of John and Sarah's love for each other, from behind until now. Behind, you can see how foolish we all can act sometimes. But looking at today's picture, you can see that love doesn't give up, but is always willing to try again. You both are also a good example of how love is willing to begin fresh, even after disaster entered your life Jack, with the loss of your parents. Two couples and two examples of pain and despair, yet love comes out as a conqueror by being willing to take a fresh start at life again. I have been waiting to see the day of your marriage, Jack, and I am so happy that I can be part of it in person."

"Me too, Uma. I wasn't sure if my heart would ever find someone strong enough to marry. The news of my parents' death brought some dark days with emotional confusion about life and its purpose. Yet what's amazing to me is that in the midst of all that, love still found me and changed my way of thinking. Something that I thought would never happen actually happened. The love Kalyani and I have always had for each other became complete the day I returned, even though my heart was full of despair. In that moment love transformed into happiness. I had always dreamed of having Kalyani.

"Another thing that amazes me is the timing. Who could time it and be at the right place at the right time unless God Almighty Himself made it happen? My faith in God tells me that there is no luck. Nothing just happens. If we could live a life through luck then there would be no need for a living God to change things."

Uma turned to Kalyani and asked her, "What do you have to say about this?"

"My faith tells me that life is not built on our own timing but on God's alone, who is eternal. I must say that it makes a big difference in life, to have someone to love and who loves you in return, to know that you have someone fighting alongside and encouraging you not to give up."

After Kaylani spoke those words, Uma looked up into the sky where dark clouds were approaching. Uma shouted to everyone in the field, "Today's workday is over a little earlier because of the bad weather coming. Let's all go to our houses and we will continue tomorrow if the weather is okay."

Everyone went home and Kalyani, Jack, and Uma went to the guesthouse to continue enjoying each other's company. While Kalyani and Jack took turns showering and getting cleaned up, Uma prepared food for dinner. When they were finished getting ready, Kalyani and Jack joined Uma in the kitchen.

Uma looked at Jack and said to him, "Would you like to cook dinner tonight along with your wife-to-be?"

"It depends on what kind of food you want us to cook," he answered.

With a smile, Uma said, "What about pasta? Spaghetti with meat sauce?"

Jack looked at Kalyani and said, "I am willing to help if you can teach me how you make it."

"My love, I would love to show you how to cook so next time you can make it on your own, as my husband."

Uma said, "As you can see, I already have everything on the kitchen counter, so while I shower, you can both begin to cook dinner. I believe that our friends will be home shortly."

After Uma closed the door and began to take a shower, Jack hugged Kalyani and said, "Isn't it great to cook dinner together?"

"Yes Jack, it's great. Every day that we spend doing things together helps me realize what a blessed woman I am to marry a man like you. I know that there will be days of struggle, but to know that you will be by my side always makes my heart shout in happiness."

"Thank you, my love, for such nice words. My heart is so happy that I feel like screaming for joy because of the life I have and knowing that I can share it with you, Kalyani."

The front door opened and through it entered John, Flower, and Sarah from their day in the jungle together. John said, "How nice to come home hungry and see the two lovebirds cooking dinner together. What are you cooking? It smells very good."

"We are cooking pasta."

Jack asked Sarah, "How was your first elephant ride in the jungle?"

"It was the greatest adventure to know that there were wild animals surrounding us on every side, but the biggest one of them all was right beneath us to protect us. In spite of all this, I'm glad that I had the courage to go through with it. It was a step of faith to explore something new in my life, and I am very glad to have shared this experience with Flower. If I had stayed home, I would have never seen the beauty of the flowers that Flower had arranged on her own. Your sister truly has a great gift of making flowers stand out and look their best in the light."

Sarah continued, "I would say that humans value appearance. Just like a flower, which needs to look good and inviting to be picked, placed in a vase, and nourished with living water to fill its roots so that it can continue to look and feel its best for the short time of its life. Then this flower is able to live and fulfill its purpose to look beautiful.

"It's the same with people. We were created to look our best by being our best, and that is our purpose in life, to make a difference in someone else's life. This is not easy to achieve. That's why God wrote the Bible for His people to follow and obey, which teaches us how to live our lives. Read it to be wise, believe it to be safe, and practice it. It contains light to guide you, food to support you, and comfort to cheer you. It is the traveler's map, the pilgrim's staff, the pilot's compass, the soldier's sword, and the Christian's charter.

"Read it slowly, frequently, and pray. Just like a child is eager to do the same things as his or her parents, we should be eager to be like our Father. Parents feed their child's soul, by allowing them to experience different emotions, until they are a mature age and are able to stand on their own feet for the first time.

"Though I am not a parent yet, I must say from my own experience that we can all make a tremendous impact on each other's lives by the way we live and express ourselves emotionally from the depths of ourselves. And where do our emotions come from, if not from feelings logged into our memory bank of past experiences? We live through situations presented in our lives and learn from them.

"Just like the flower, we all need living water to stay whole and unbroken, not destroyed from running low on fuel. But our fuel is not like the flower's fuel, water. It is something more vital. And if you are honest and understanding, you know that I am talking about love. For a flower doesn't have a soul like we do. When you drink water, do you become happy while drinking it? Of course not. We need water to live and for our bodies to function right. But a happy and joyful life needs your heart to be filled with a kind of love that you can trust. But to be honest with you all, how can I trust anyone when I can't trust myself to keep from messing up and making mistakes?

"That's why I trust God alone. No one else can pick me up when I fall, because I know that God knows my heart and that I am doing my best every day."

Flower cut in and said, "I love you, Sarah. I am so blessed to know that you and John love God like I love Him. I am especially blessed to have new, great parents whom I love dearly. I know that we will all have a good life together with equal love for one another."

"Oh, Flower, thank you so much for saying that. I wondered if you would ever be able to say those words to me, since I am not your real mother. I'm sorry, Flower, but I can't hold back these tears of joy any longer and I need to give you a hug."

While Sarah hugged her, she whispered into Flower's ear, "I am so happy. It feels like I'm dreaming. I was afraid the day to be a mother would never come. But because you love me, I can be a mother today and live with you and my loving husband. So I just want to say thank you, Flower, for loving me."

"Well, thank you, Sarah. Loving you comes easy for me, because you are a wonderful and loving person. I am glad that I can fill the spot for your missing child and be part of a family that you and John have been waiting for. So, let's enjoy this wonderful dinner that my brother and his wife-to-be have made for us."

They all enjoyed the dinner more knowing that everyone's heart was full of love for each other and that the day of the wedding was approaching very quickly. There was only one day left before the wedding and the harvest party would take a place.

Though none of the family members were working, they all woke up early to have breakfast together as usual. After breakfast they began to organize for the big celebration that would take place the following day up on the hill beside Flower and Jack's new house. They all stood outside trying to plan where to put all of the tables and chairs and where to install the dance floor. Suddenly, who should pull up in a big truck, if not the wedding planners themselves?

The planning for the tables was put on hold for a bit, once everyone was told that all the wedding clothes were done and ready to be tried on individually. The men were quick to try their outfits for the wedding. They returned to help with moving and arranging tables, chairs and putting together the dance floor for the wedding.

The women, however, came back two hours later and everything was complete. It doesn't matter how old a woman becomes, a day of looking like a princess is always welcomed and enjoyed like it was the first time. For most women, their wedding day is the most important day of all. It is a day that will be remembered by many people for a long time, and that's why it's so important to make it special.

The good thing for Jack and Kalyani's wedding was that they had many dear friends who'd already been through their own weddings who could share their insight and what they thought was important to know.

After a long and exhausting day of planning, as the last daylight approached, everyone went to bed with big expectations of a wonderful wedding and harvest party to be held the next day. To make it harder for Kalyani and Jack, they were not allowed to see each other until the wedding, when Jack's wife-to-be would walk up the aisle to face Jack and become his love for a lifetime.

So Jack and John slept for the night at the new house. Uma, Flower, Kalyani, and Sarah slept at the guesthouse.

They Are No Longer Two But One

The day that everyone was waiting for had finally arrived. Sarah left the guesthouse and went to see her husband. She knocked on the door and walked inside and saw John and Jack, who were already up and smiling.

Sarah informed John, "It was a very restless night for all of us who slept in the guesthouse. Kalyani is so nervous about getting married."

Jack said, "What do you mean she's nervous?"

"Ah, don't be silly, Jack. Of course Kalyani wants to marry you. She's just nervous about how many people are attending the wedding. There will be close to one hundred people and Kalyani is nervous about something going wrong, like, slipping and fall in her wedding dress. Don't worry Jack, she will be alright as soon as the wedding ceremony begins. If I remember right, I was a nervous wreck myself before our wedding ceremony."

John looked outside to see if the weather was looking good and said, "Your wedding day is starting out great, Jack. The wedding wouldn't be so beautiful without good weather."

Then John looked at his wife, gave her a smile, and said. "I don't know why, but I feel nervous too. Maybe it's because we were apart for so long. We've both changed for the better during this time of loneliness. In a way, it feels like we are getting married all over again."

Sarah looked at her husband and said, "I feel the same way. So let's pretend that we are getting married again. After all, we've been granted a new life with a complete family."

"Come here, Sarah. I need to give you a hug as my new wife."

While John and Sarah hugged each other, Jack was jealous and said, "This isn't fair. I want to hug Kalyani also."

Sarah told Jack, "Be patient and remember that on this day, Kalyani will look her best for you."

"Forgive me for being childish, Sarah, I'm just so anxious for the moment when I get to say, 'This is my wife.' It must be a great feeling to say those words."

"Yes, without a doubt, it's the best feeling in the world. Sarah has chosen me to be her partner for life and to grow old together as a couple. What a blessed man I am. Aren't we all being shaped and molded into who we truly are by what we've been through in life?

"What is also important is who we meet along the path of life and who we allow to be part of our life. So what is easier, to love or to hate? Or should I say, which one feels better in your heart? By loving each other in how we talk and act, others will be influenced to do the same. A word that is spoken can lift someone up or break someone down."

John continued, "We have something in common, Jack. We've both known them since we were young. But enough about me and Sarah, for this day is about you and Kalyani becoming husband and wife and I know in my heart that we will spend many happy days together as friends and married couples."

"Thank you for such encouraging words about marriage. I also know in my heart that we will be friends forever."

At that moment Sarah said to both men, "Let's do our very best today to make sure that Kalyani has a great and beautiful day, as she becomes a wife to Jack. Another thing, on my way over here, I noticed someone was up early and working hard to make this day extra beautiful with wild flowers for the wedding. I believe Flower would appreciate a helping hand."

When John and Jack went to Flower she said, "I want this day to be the most beautiful day of Kalyani's life. The wedding planner has made a beautiful flower arrangement for Jack and Kalyani's table only. But I would like to make it more beautiful by having flowers at every table. We have twelve tables that need flower arrangements, and as you can see, I don't have enough flowers to make it happen. I only have enough for two tables, but I need flowers for ten more tables. John, do you remember the path we took to the temple?"

"Yes Flower, I remember."

"At the beginning of the trail you will find all the flowers we need."

John looked at Flower and asked her, "Is it okay if we take Toby along with us into the jungle?"

"Of course. He will keep you safe and he knows the trail well."

Flower directed Toby to go with Jack and John into the jungle.

Back at the guesthouse, the ladies were having fun together on this special day.

The wedding ceremony would begin at four o'clock. They only had six hours to get ready. The women prepared for the wedding by making each other's hair look its best.

There would be a Baptist pastor to present the wedding vows. He was set to arrive at three o'clock. John, the best man, along with Jack, Uma, Sarah, and Flower would stand at the altar, waiting for the bride to walk up to her groom.

John and Jack returned with the flowers.

"Thank you so much for your help! I never would have been able to complete every table with flowers if it weren't for you."

Jack then asked Flower, "Do you like idea of making a few fires tonight, when it's dark, to give light and to keep insects away?"

Flower agreed with Jack's idea. John and Jack collected some firewood beside the shed next to the guesthouse. They made four stacks in different locations within the party grounds.

After they finished collecting all the wood and putting it in place, John and Jack went to shower before dressing for the wedding. With only one hour left, people started to arrive for the wedding and harvest party.

Everyone in the family was almost ready for the wedding. Flower walked in to join the women, who were upset with her for being so late.

Flower replied, "I'm sorry from being so late, but there was something I had to do personally for the wedding to be complete. You don't know what I'm referring to right now, but you will later. Let me hurry up to take a shower and then you can help me look beautiful." Flower jumped into the shower and the people continued to gather for the wedding.

John walked outside from the house and directed people to the tables in order to be seated while waiting for the bride. The pastor already stood at the altar.

Everyone was surprised when an orchestra walked around the wedding altar. John had arranged, in total secret, for an orchestra to play live music for the wedding.

Everyone who was attending the wedding was in place. Kalyani opened the door leading out from the guesthouse. All eyes were fixed on her beauty. She looked stunning, wearing a light blue silk dress. Her bouquet was full of many beautiful white orchids, with one red orchid in the middle representing her heart full of love for the man she was walking toward, who would be her husband.

As Kalyani walked outside, she was surprised by the live music playing. She felt the music reach into her soul and she couldn't hold back the tears of joy any longer. Her nervousness left her and she was filled with a kind of peace like she'd never felt before in her heart.

Jack looked at Kalyani and thought to himself, "I have never seen a more beautiful bride in my whole life. I have never seen so many feelings expressed on someone's face as right now on Kalyani's face. To see my wife-to-be walking toward me, with a shy smile on her face, yet at the same time with tears streaming down her cheeks... makes me realize that complete happiness is when you can share all of the love in your heart with tears of joy.

Jack looked around and noticed that Kalyani was not the only one crying. Many guests were crying as the music reached their hearts. Knowing that they cried tears of happiness for two people finding each other made Jack tear up as well.

Kalyani walked up to Jack and put her red flower of love into his chest pocket, located on the side of his heart. They continued to share tears of joy with each other. The pastor asked Jack to read his personal wedding vows to Kalyani. Jack wiped the tears from his face, reached into his chest pocket inside the jacket, and pulled out his love note.

Before he began to read, Jack and Kalyani looked into each other's eyes and enjoyed the moment together, sharing tears from hearts full of joy.

Jack got a hold of himself and, keeping back his tears of joy, opened his lips and began to speak his personal vow of love for Kalyani.

Love Like Nothing Else

"Kalyani, with these words spoken from the deepest part of myself, my heart, I hope you will understand the love that I have always had for you while growing up. Today my dream for you and I to come together as a husband and wife has become reality.

"Time passed and the sweet way you treated me while we were growing up brought new dreams and hopes that my heart had never before explored. My feelings for you became limited the day I joined the navy. My fear of losing you to someone else while I was gone really tormented my heart. I desired to tell you my true intentions, my feelings regarding you and who I wanted you to be in my life. I left you alone a young girl and came back after three years to see and receive a woman.

"I realize today that God has favored me with His blessing: to receive you as my wife. To me, you are more than a wife. You are an angel sent from above to complete my love. So with these words, Kalyani, I hope that you understand all that my heart feels for you. I love you, Kalyani."

Kalyani agreed with Jack and said, "I love you, Jack."

At that moment the pastor looked at Flower and

nodded for her to step forward to stand in front of the altar, facing the people. She began to read from the Bible, the love chapter, 1 Corinthians 13:1-13:

"If I speak in tongues of men and of angels, but have not love, I am only a resounding gong or a clanging cymbal. If I have the gift of prophecy and can fathom all mysteries and all knowledge, and if I have faith that can move mountains, but have not love, I am nothing. If I give all I possess to the poor and surrender my body to the flames, but have not love, I gain nothing.

"Love is patient, love is kind. It does not envy, it does not boast, it is not proud. It is not rude, it is not self-seeking, it is not easily angered, it keeps no record of wrongs. Love does not delight in evil but rejoices with the truth. It always protects, always trusts, always hopes, always perseveres. Love never fails. But where there are prophecies, they will cease; where there are tongues, they will be stilled; where there is knowledge, it will pass away. For we know in part and we prophesy in part, but when perfection comes, the imperfect disappears.

"When I was a child, I talked like a child; I thought like a child, I reasoned like a child. When I became a man, I put childish ways behind me. Now we see but a poor reflection as in a mirror; then we shall see face-to-face. Now I know in part; then I shall know fully, even as I am fully known. And now these three remain: faith, hope and love. But the greatest of these is love."

After Flower was done reading, the pastor turned to Kalyani and Jack and asked them both to say their oaths to each other.

When this was done and the rings were placed on

each other, the pastor said to Jack, "You may kiss the bride, since you are husband and wife by the witness of God."

Jack kissed Kalyani for the first time, as her husband. A moment later they were both dancing their first dance as a married couple. When their dance was over, the celebration opened for everyone to enjoy, to celebrate their marriage. With lots of good food to eat and music to dance to, there was much happiness for this newlywed couple, as well as for a successful harvest together as a big happy family.

The wedding and harvest party continued into the late hours of the night. The party was stopped by rain and everyone went home, to sleep with satisfied hearts because of Jack and Kalyani's marriage.

A Friend Who Will Be Missed

The morning after the wedding, everyone slept late, except Flower. She got up early and looked for Toby, who never left her sight if it could be helped. For the first time ever, Flower was concerned about Toby, wondering where he'd gone without her.

Flower ran into the guesthouse, yelling in a panic, waking John up with the noise. Worried, Flower said, "Something is wrong! Toby has never left alone without being quick to come back. Oh John, hurry up! I have a bad feeling that something horrible has happened to Toby."

"Calm down, Flower, and take it easy. I'm sure that there's an explanation for why he isn't back yet."

"Please John, I need you to come with me to look for Toby. I've never been so troubled before about where he might be."

Sarah overheard the conversation and said to Flower, "Let's go together and find your elephant."

Sarah and John got dressed and, along with Flower, started to search for Toby by entering the trail that led into the jungle. All three were walking in the jungle and looking for Toby when Sarah asked Flower, "What makes you think that something bad has happened to Toby?"

"I can't explain why, I just have a bad feeling in my heart right now. I just know that something is wrong and I will not stop worrying until I know the truth regarding my best friend."

In that moment they heard a gunshot and their concern for Toby grew. They began to run toward the sound of the gunshot. A few moments later, their chase ended with the sound of a commotion among people not far from where they were. They walked into a crowd of people who blocked the view to all the commotion.

Flower was the first to push through the crowd and saw that Toby was the reason for the upset crowd. The eyes of Toby and Flower connected as one, like the first time they met. She saw that Toby was stuck in a hole again, but this time it was more serious. Flower understood that Toby was in a serious situation. This time he couldn't be saved because he was badly wounded. He was dying. She ran over and grabbed his trunk.

Flower was shocked to see only the top of Toby's head. To be even with the ground meant his body lay in a deep hole, which poachers had dug to capture tigers. Instead of catching a tiger, Toby had fallen in. During the fall, Toby was stabbed in the chest by a point-tipped branch that had been angled for a tiger to fall upon.

Flower didn't know what to feel. For the moment, she and Toby were saying goodbye to each other in silence. While Toby held onto Flower's hand, a man of the crowd spoke up and made it even harder for Flower to grasp what had just happened to her.

"That elephant is dying and there is no need to try and help him."

John approached the man and said, "Excuse me sir, but the elephant belongs to the girl you're talking to, so you could show some compassion."

The man fell on his knees beside Flower, put his hand on her shoulder and said, "Oh child, I am so sorry for my selfish words. Please forgive me. I guess I'm shocked to see that this has happened in our area. Poachers. They only kill animals to make money on their skins and tusks and to sell them illegally."

Flower nodded at the man and accepted his apology. Sarah and John joined Flower and her troubled heart and said goodbye together to their dying friend, Toby the elephant.

After sharing tears together for a while, John asked Flower, "Where do you want Toby to be buried?"

"If it's possible John, I would like to have him buried next to my house by the edge of the jungle."

"Consider it done, Flower." At that same moment, Sarah called on her cellphone to the ranger's office to find out if Toby could be buried where Flower desired. John, Sarah, and Flower began their walk back home. It wasn't that long but it felt that way, because no one said a word. Their hearts shared the loss of a good friend, a friend who couldn't be replaced.

A while later, Sarah opened the door leading into the guesthouse and walked inside together with John and Flower. Sarah made some tea for them and sat by the kitchen table, reflecting on what had happened.

John said to Flower, "I don't know what to say in

words about Toby and the way he left us. My heart feels so sad for you right now. First, losing your parents the way you did and now losing your dear friend as well, in a way that is hard for us to accept."

Flower hadn't been able to stop crying since she'd left Toby for good. With tears stuck in her throat she said, "John, I don't want to be here any longer, for everyone that I've cared for has gone and died. Please John, take me away from this place. I need closure for my heart in a place where I haven't been hurt. Where my heart can find hope to live again. I've never been away from my country before, but today I am ready to take a chance, since there is nothing left in my heart for this place anymore. Take me to England."

Flower looked at Sarah, with an expression they'd never seen on her face before, and said, "Sarah, I would love to meet your family back home in England."

"Come here, Flower, I need a hug. Personally, I wish we were on an airplane right now. Until we receive the adoption papers, your brother is your legal guardian. In order for John and I to take you with us, he must agree with your request first. You have your passport, but we still need a written statement from your brother saying that we can take you with us to England."

Being so anxious to leave, Flower suggested that Sarah and John go and ask for her brother's approval right away.

"Flower, I want you to wait here while we go and talk to your brother. We will inform him about your request."

After a long hour of tears and sadness over his sister, and with a compassionate heart, Jack approved Flower's request by signing the papers. Sarah ran back to Flower and shared the good news.

At the same time, John said to Jack, "Thank you for being so understanding of Flower and her feelings right now, because of what has happened to her dear friend Toby." Then he also said, "I will return and make sure that the plans of making this town into a better place, by building its own school, will happen."

Sarah ordered the airplane tickets while John and Jack were still talking about the future of this town and its people.

Two days later, John, Sarah, and Flower were sitting on the plane, on their way to England. None of their family members had any idea who was coming home as a complete family with a little girl.

On the airplane, Flower thought about her future. She felt excited to leave her old life and bad memories and to begin a new life with a new family in a foreign country, England. With one hand, John held Sarah's and in the other, Flower's.

For the first time in John's life, he felt complete. He knew that he was on his way to building a family. Which he'd been longing to do for a long time.

John felt like the happiest man on earth.